FALLING LIKE STARS

Jenny Tincher

CONTENTS

CHAPTER 1

Ezra Parker was ephemeral, just fleeting enough to become a memory. How entropic is memory, its ability to change mundane experiences into hazy, dreamlike spring days, so mystical and songlike that I question if they ever happened. In those days with Ezra, I found everything I could have ever wanted—and the heartache that I once cherished as elements of fiction became my temporary truth. Inevitably, I realized that the world is filled with people carrying knives, though with the purest of intentions.

We fall in love not with people, Narnie, but with moments, he would say. Love is nothing more than a drug, an intoxicant, and eventually all intoxicants wear off, don't they?

A cautionary tale, gentle in even his cruelty—but there was something about him that made even the most stubborn of hearts surrender to his nuances.

"Ezra Parker?" repeated the elderly woman behind the registration desk at Holden High. A new semester was beginning after the end of an awfully torrid summer—and here I was, two spots behind him in line, waiting to receive my schedule. "You must be new if you're a Parker," she continued, scavenging the stack of files surrounding her. "We haven't registered anybody with that name, hon. Are you sure your parents finished the paperwork?"

He looked directly ahead.

She glanced sheepishly at her coworker before facing Ezra once again. "Why don't we call your family, hon?"

"I can't do that, Ms. Liebson."

The woman, Ms. Liebson, scrunched her face in confusion. "Are you sure? Are they at work or something? I am sure we can find at least one person of contact," she trailed off—but when she made the call moments later to his home, a dated voicemail greeted her on the other end of the line.

"I heard his parents are dead," Anita Karki whispered to her friend, Lolita Akbar, just a step behind me. "But apparently he still pays their phone carrier just to hear his Mama's voice."

"Who is your guardian, Ezra?" Ms. Liebson asked him, her expression softening.

"I—uh..."

"You haven't got anybody? No relatives or anything?"

He looked down at his feet.

Ms. Liebson narrowed her eyes at us before referring him to the headmaster's office. As he brushed past me in that crowded hour, I wanted to ask him a million questions, but he left in a haste, leaving behind a trail of his presence in the air, a similarly brooding demeanor and his subtle smile.

I saw him again two days later as I was trying out for cheerleading on the two acres of sparse land behind Holden High. With Coach Washington hosting football tryouts alongside us, the majority of the space had been sanctioned off for the footballers with large orange cones. Ezra was sitting on the bleachers in his football gear, his head tucked into the pages of Viktor Frankl's Man's Search for Meaning.

Every day in that hour, before Coach Washington blew his whistle to signal the beginning of tryouts, he would sit there just like that: with his head buried in the pages of dilapidated library books: de Beauvoir after Frankl, and then Seneca. Stranded in the world of fiction and its many mysteries, he paid no heed to the chaos we created for him to see—but I saw him. His shy glances. His periodic sighs. His quickening blinks as his body was cast in darkness by a floating cloud—the conviction with which he carried himself.

Maybe he was asking for it: for me to be captivated. I even picked up Hermann Hesse one evening after seeing Siddhartha poking out of his duffel bag. It was then that he approached me, with that same unwavering conviction. "Good choice," he said, motioning towards the battered copy of Siddhartha perched between my fingers. "Narnie, right? Have you seen Coach Washington?"

I looked up at him dumbly, pathetically—longingly. "Yeah."

"Yeah?"

I quickly shook my head. "Wait, no."

Amused, he raised an eyebrow. "No?"

"No, sorry," I said again.

He thanked me, leaving without another word.

I thought about him for days.

Beyond his arresting glance and the fading birthmark beneath his eye, his passion was his intrigue—and boys like him were inevitably the subject of great fascination, because Sol Flores captivated him before I could. I jogged into the field one day to find that he had company on his forth step on the bleachers. As I walked past the two, I was overcome by the sound of their quiet conversation. By chance then, our eyes met again.

He bit into the apple on his hand, winking innocently, and my cheeks burnt to a crisp.

Chapter 2

There was an unsettling homogeneity to the names of the girls enlisted to Holden's cheerleading team: Ashley Bennett, Hannah Ricco, Liza Smith...and eventually me, Narnie Larson. My name was on the very bottom of the list, written in dark cursive and plastered on a bulletin in front of the school. The incandescence of the sun blanketed the several acres of our school property, shining with even more intensity on the paper, which, I soon observed, had a series of clumsily erased question marks after my name.

I stared at the paper, wondering why those marks were there, until the bell rang, signaling the beginning of class. When I came back several hours later, I was still Narnie Larson with large, daunting question marks after my name.

I learned from Lolita Akbar one day in the girls' locker room that the question marks were there because Sol herself had reservations about me. "And it probably has to do with the fact that Ezra Parker can't get his eyes off of you," she said, drying her wet hair with her towel.

I closed my locker, Lolita's words ringing in my ears. I could not process that I was somebody worth looking at by anybody, much less Ezra Parker.

It took terse conversations with the girls in between classes to discover that suburbia was stranger than Lolita had let on. Its peacefulness distracted from its chaos, its golden exterior of prosperity disguising the deceptiveness of the people within—and Sol was the most deceptive of them all. She stood out like a black swan for her forced expressions when she approached me after practice that day. "Narnie, right?" she asked nonchalantly.

I thought about Lolita's words as I upheld my own deceptive front. "Sol."

"That's me."

I smiled weakly, not knowing what else to do.

"Welcome to the team," she said. "I've been hearing a lot about you these days. From Coach Choi, you know? She has been going on and on about your flexibility."

I looked at Coach Choi, who was speaking to two of our girls, before meeting Sol's gaze once again. "Oh, really?"

"Yeah. You were super impressive at tryouts."

"I did a lot of dancing back in San City. It's just a part of the transition, I guess."

Sol seemed unfazed by my response, as if she had been anticipating it all along. "Yeah, quite the transition. You are now officially condemned to the middle of nowhere like the rest of us."

I met her eye, laughing a little.

Sol bit her lip, motioning her head toward the other side of the field. "See him, Narnie? The one with the blonde hair? That's Anderson Flemming. He's holding a little gathering at his place tonight to celebrate the new season. I'm sure he wouldn't mind if you were my plus one."

Lolita flickered through my mind and I suddenly itched to question Sol's friendliness, but I mustered a smile, embracing my confidence despite my feeling of displacement. "I'll be there."

Anderson Flemming lived in a two acre estate on the border of Holden and Port Orion, where the only sound you could hear for the next twenty miles was the hum of your own breathing. Confined to the silence of suburbia, my mind wandered to the days when it was not just Mama and I, fending off the wilderness on our own. In some memories, we are sitting on our veranda, biting back tears as we exchange a spoonful of Papa's rhubarb pie. I'll be home soon, baby, he had said. More than a year later, we were still waiting for him to come home.

I dropped the thought as 4 Mulberry Drive manifested before me. People streamed in and out of the front door, jostling for space atop the front lawn. I exited my car, searching the crowd for a familiar face or two.

"Narnie!"

I gave a start, turning around. "Sol, hi!"

She was holding a red plastic cup on one hand and Anderson Flemming on the other. "Okay so, Narnie meet Anderson. Anderson, Narnie."

I examined him quietly, taking in the mellowness with which he carried himself.

"Well, guys, don't just stand there!" she said, pulling us closer together.

I extended a hand, but Anderson drew me into a hug. "Welcome to Holden, Narnie."

"Thanks, thanks," I said, pulling away.

Sol giggled. "Come on. We'll introduce you to the others."

As she led us through swarms of indistinguishable faces, I regretted not bringing a sweater. We walked until we ran into Mateo

White, a shy, brown haired boy and Sol's oldest friend, and then Ezra himself. A small smile graced Ezra Parker's face when he saw me. "Narnie Larson," he said a matter-of-factly, as if he had been saying it all his life.

"Hi Ezra—Mateo," I greeted, giving the two a brief smile.

We lost ourselves in small talk as Sol left to fetch us sangria, taking Anderson with her. In between sips of beer, Mateo asked me about San City and its horror stories. "How does it feel to call that place home, Narnie? Did you consider San City your home?"

I thought back to the fleeting nights by the Hudson, trying to find answers in a city saturated by the dampness of after rain. I thought about my best friend, Trevor, who I hadn't seen since that day in late August when Mama packed both of our bags and brought us here. No, I did not consider San City my home. But those timeless moments with the people I loved the most—that was home.

"Maybe I'll find myself in a place like that one day," Mateo continued. Being stuck in one place for all of his life was his condemnation. It was all of theirs.

"It was home in some way," I said. "You should visit."

"Maybe I will."

It was then that his phone rang. He excused himself, leaving just Ezra and I. Ezra was quicker on his feet than I was, carrying himself with a calmness I always lacked. "Finish Siddhartha yet?"

I tried to tame the butterflies in my stomach at his words. "Almost."

"It's beautiful, isn't it? How Sid turns the unbearable pain of living into laughter—into a joke. How humor ends up being his liberation."

"Of course, Ezra, isn't that kind of the meaning of life?" I said cheekily, but in my head, I was already in the sky. I was in a world untouched by the business of carnal, adolescent commotion, where the stench of alcohol and sweat no longer saturated the air, but the possibility of everything Ezra and I could be did.

Unrealistic and impractical in love, my horoscope had read, just this morning.

Ezra leaned forward, his eyes meeting mine. "You want to get out of here?"

And the butterflies swarmed, floating all around.

"Sure," I finally said.

Love was not supposed to plant its seed then, in Anderson Flemming's backyard. It was not supposed to grow in our moments of exaltation over passages of unfinished books, or, minutes later, on his battered Harley overseeing the suburban vista with trees awning before us, like a tunnel to paradise. The moment unraveled in waves, with the crisp wind blowing on my face as I held him on the backseat of his motorcycle, riding through Holden, its jungles and lightless roads: the byproduct of imprudent decisions and adolescent longing.

Ezra parked his Harley by an overlook on the side of the highway. We sat on the flattest surface we could find and let our feet dangle on the edge of the precipice. He removed a layer of his jacket and draped it around me. "Favorite season?"

I recoiled into it, taking in the soft smell of his lavender softener. "Thank you, Ezra."

"You seemed cold."

"I was. Just a little bit."

"Just a little?"

I laughed, just a little. "It's autumn. My favorite season is autumn."

"Autumn. Suits you."

"I take it you're not an autumn kind of guy?"

"My mom," he began with a smile. "Her favorite season was autumn."

My heart trembled for him, for the way his face briefly gave into his melancholy as he spoke about his mother in the past tense. "And yours?" I asked him softly.

"Summer," he said without a moment's thought.

"You've thought about this before."

"Maybe just a little."

"Just a little?" I teased him, laughing.

He laughed too.

As his laughter died down, I crossed my legs and faced him. "Okay so, why summer?"

"Summer is when I feel the most free. And the longer days give me the illusion of immortality."

My heart fluttered uncontrollably as he continued. "I feel like everyone's favorite season tells us a lot about who they are. It's like every season has this collectively understood personality. We associate summer with happiness, pleasure and liberation, while we associate winter with the opposite. I don't know. Maybe there's an element of nostalgia to it. I've always loved the summer because it holds some of my most beautiful memories."

"What are some of your most beautiful memories, Ezra?"

He paused as if I had caught him off guard. "And suddenly I can't remember any of my good memories."

I laughed. "Maybe your idea is only good in theory."

He laughed too, scratching his temples. "Wow."

"Yeah?"

"I guess my parents come to mind," he said. "They were university professors, so they always had the summers off. Every June, we would drive down to Vemlich Park and ride the rollercoasters until the nausea hit. The days were so long, Narnie. It was like they would never end, like time slowed down and you could fit eternity in an hour if you tried.

"And then, just riding the Harley with my sister's boyfriend, Alex, before he turned out to be the scum of the century. Smoking a shit ton of pot and falling in love for the first time. The magic I felt then, like I wasn't made of flesh and bone and nothing could touch me." His reflective visage suddenly became somber. "I guess I'm better off not remembering all of that right now. Tell me about you—why autumn?"

"I don't have an answer as good as yours."

"Oh me? I don't know what I'm saying half of the time."

I laughed, shaking my head. "Yeah, okay, Ezra."

"I'm serious!"

I closed my eyes, inhaling the late summer breeze. The familiar smell of the eucalyptus in the air transported me to the hikes Mama, Papa and I would take in late autumn.

"Hey, you okay?"

Was I? I don't know...I guessed I missed the autumns back home—home, in San City, where things were familiar. I had a lot of theories about why Mama had brought us back here, to my father's hometown. We had no reason to leave the city. We were never particularly poor. Even when I was born prematurely, while my parents were still in university, they found creative ways to give me everything I could have wanted: a Barbie doll at the age of eight, a makeup set at thirteen and exquisite memories to leave me hollow by seventeen. Mama had gone on to become a leading human right's attorney, carrying us from our destitute one bedroom apartment in University Lane to the Upper East Side, home of the somebodies. But these days, none of that seemed to particularly matter.

When I opened my eyes again, I found my lips moving to no sound—and suddenly it was like someone had punctured my lungs, like I could no longer breathe despite feverishly gasping for air. I swallowed my words, nodding, because a simple motion of the head was easier than explaining why I wasn't.

Ezra put his hand beside mine. "Let's move on, then?"

"I'd like that," I said, but suddenly, all I could feel was the friction generated by the one inch of proximity separating our fingers.

Ezra's dream was to become a federal prosecutor. He had a restless fascination with the law that seemed deeper than a mere interest in bureaucratic procedure. "I want to study philosophy and then go onto law school. Then start out my professional career as a lawyer or go into clerkship, if I manage to convince the world that I am not as mediocre as I appear."

"You're not mediocre, Ezra."

"How do you know, Narnie? You just met me."

I looked away, not knowing what to say.

"What about you?" he digressed. "Any five year plans?"

I shook my head, stretching my feet. "Nope. Not all of us know ourselves as well as you do."

"Had a little too much time to soul search, I guess."

"I've had the same amount of time. Why don't I know myself yet?"

"Clearly you just need to get on my level."

"Clearly."

I laughed, just a little. And we stayed there until I noticed I had three missed calls from Mama. Ezra understood immediately—and we rode back to Mulberry Drive on Ezra's Harley. He dropped me by my car.

Mama was already in bed by the time I arrived home, snoring lightly. From my bedroom window, I watched the violet sky fade into the soothing glimmer of dawn.

I had once read in a novel that the word nostalgia has its origins in a Greek word, nostos, signifying a call to return home. As I stood under the moonlight, my seventeen year old self, consumed by the intoxication led on by Ezra Parker, I took in the feeling of a rising nostalgia: of then returning to a home I never knew existed. Maybe we find home at forty when we begin paying off a mortgage or maybe we find it years in advance, when we come across love for the very first time. In the moments that followed, I let myself forget that Ezra Parker was still a stranger. I let myself believe that I was on a path home at last.

CHAPTER 3

I awoke the next morning in a haze. Dawn broke slowly into morning—and I realized through my hammering heart that last night had been more than a mirage. The smell of cardamom greeted me in the kitchen, where Nana was, brewing tea and skimming The Holden Sun. A cautionary look overtook her face as she skimmed an article headlined Mysterious disappearances continue around Holden, targeting young girls.

"Morning Nana," I said, walking into the kitchen.

She frowned, putting the newspaper down. "Long night?"

"I was at Anderson Flemming's party," I explained sheepishly. I grabbed the kettle from the stovetop and poured myself a cup of tea. "Do you know Anderson Flemming?"

"They're good people, the Flemmings," she said, allowing herself to soften. "Just let us know if you'll be home late next time, Narnie. Maya was worried sick. Said you wouldn't pick up her calls. You know how she is these days."

I nodded. Nana was right: Mama was more alert than usual these days. Papa's death had done that to her. It had made her fragile.

Death was funny in that regard. It had weakened all of us, targeting Mama's romantic soul just as indiscriminately as my dispassionate one. Until Papa was its victim, it had been a mere abstraction—the distant plight Middle Eastern children or strangers in fleeting news reports. But then it happened to him, arriving abruptly, vehemently, unsuspectingly—and that was the most haunting of all, the realization that he too was condemned to this dreadful end. A man we had once believed to be immortal, today, all of his passions, artifacts and convictions were in the process of withering into a state of nonbeing. And here we were in the aftermath, plagued with the ambiguity of being alive, condemned to live until we died.

Nana pointed to a plate of scrambled eggs on the counter, her eyes meeting mine. "Eat."

I finished my breakfast in silence, ruminating about Papa as I often did. I wanted nothing more than for him to walk through the front door, to tease us as he often would, to tell us, Did you really believe that I could die? You silly girls.

"Hurry, darling," Nana said, pulling me away from my thoughts. "You'll be late."

"Love you, Nan," I said, finishing my last sip of tea. I kissed her goodbye before leaving for the day. Outside, Mrs. Henry, our neighbor, was exiting her house with her daughter, Isabella.

"Morning Mrs. Henry," I said, walking into our driveway.

"Narnie," she said warmly. "It's so nice to see you, dear. I was just dropping Isabella off at school. Do you need a ride?"

Her ride was a beaten Cooper old enough to have been her ancestor's. My eyes wandered from its dilapidated frame to her daughter, Isabella, who wearing a teal sweater I recognized all too well: one from Rosalie's by Marin and Chapel Street in San City, handcrafted in Merino wool. Papa had given me the same sweater two winters ago for Christmas, but in magenta.

"Actually, would Isabella want to come with?" I asked, motioning to my car.

"Hell yeah," she began, while Mrs. Henry said, "I don't know, Narnie...I wouldn't want to inconvenience you."

Isabella rolled her eyes. "Yeah, yeah. Bye Mom!"

I couldn't help but laugh as she loaded herself into my car. It was as I was sliding in beside her that Mr. Henry appeared onto their veranda. "Nice to see you again, Narnie," he said.

My body slackened all at once. I swallowed my nostalgia whole, shouting a weak "You too, Mr. Henry," before attempting to start my car, to no avail. Unfazed by my sudden shakiness, Isabella leaned over and helped me insert the key into ignition—and suddenly it was like we had known each other for years, like we weren't two strangers left alone in a chilly car.

"Thank god for you, Narnie," she said as I pulled us out of the driveway. "Mom's been so anal about driving me around these days, with the disappearances and all. Honestly, it's so embarrassing."

"She's so cute."

"Cute? More like crazy."

I laughed a little.

"Can I turn on the radio?" she asked. She didn't wait for my answer before tuning the dial to a local station playing Pinkish Sunrise by The Bodhisattvas. She did that often, I realized: ask for permission she knew she didn't need.

With the exception of our occasional chatter, the morning was relatively still. There was no rush, no people nor cars cascading in a fervent hurry to reach their destinations. I inhaled the gentle morning breeze as the nostalgic song played in the background.

The road before us could have been a pathway to a utopia. With lush magnolia trees lining every street corner, dentless sidewalks and a uniformity to every picket fence surrounding an American home, it was both serene and unsettling. I turned onto the main road, finally finding myself settling into Holden's notorious morning traffic. My heart was already hammering inside my chest when a certain green eyed boy broke the stillness. "Hey you!"

Isabella poked her head out of the window, squinting to see him. "Is that...Ezra Parker?"

I didn't need to turn around to know that it was.

"Narnie, I think he's talking to you," she said cautiously.

I unrolled the driver side window to find him on the other side. "Following me around now?"

He chuckled. "Is there anyone else more worthy of my time?"

"I don't know. Is there?"

"After last night? I'd say not."

There was a brief silence between the two of us in which we heard Isabella sigh from the passenger's seat. "Race you to school?" he finally said. The roar of his engine filled my ears before I could protest.

Isabella laughed, shaking her head. "Like we actually have a chance."

I bit my lip. As the traffic began to clear, all I could think about was Ezra Parker and what we were becoming—and this erratic restlessness in my heart as if it was at risk of falling in love for the very first time.

"So how do you know him, Narnie?" Isabella asked. She dialed down the radio until Pinkish Sunrise became a white noise fading into the background.

"We met last night at Anderson Flemming's party—do you know Anderson Flemming?"

Her face darkened, taking on an indecipherable visage. "Barely."

"Old friend?" I asked, careful not to overstep my boundaries.

"A really close old friend, once upon a time."

We arrived in the parking lot of the school then. "We don't have to talk about it, Bella," I said, parking my car. "Can I call you Bella?"

She nodded in silent gratitude, concurring to both. It was then that we spotted Ezra's Harley parked along the curb beside us. Her face recovered when she saw him leaning against it. "As if we actually had a shot of beating him."

"It was a worth a try."

She laughed. "I guess I'll leave you two to it."

"Pick you up again tomorrow morning?"

"Hell yeah. See you, Narnie."

I locked my car and headed over to Ezra's Harley, waving a final goodbye to Bella before doing so. He smiled triumphantly as I approached him. "Beat you."

I rolled my eyes. "A completely undeserved victory."

"Says who?"

"Says I."

"Nope."

"You can't just say nope all high and mighty, you cheater."

"I did not cheat."

"Cheater."

"Nope."

"Yeah, okay, whatever you say, Ezra."

We veered in the direction of the classrooms. "So where are you headed now?" he asked. Along our innocent movements, I felt my fingers gently brush his.

I bit my tongue, walking in. Entering the halls with Ezra eased my fear of displacement. The once unbearable clamor of pounding footsteps and dispersed chatter felt more distant somehow. When I saw him looking at me, awaiting a response, I recalled my schedule through my weak memory. "Existential Literature with Allen Pierre-Louis. You?"

He smiled as if my words were an act of fate. "Existential Literature with Allen Pierre-Louis."

Eight a.m existential literature with Mr. Pierre-Louis became a staple for us in the days that followed. As we navigated the ideas of Camus, Kierkegaard and Sartre, we found ourselves deeply consumed by ideas of our own, ideas we shared in post it notes. The notes came in lively colors, contrasting the otherwise humdrum suburban mornings while the trees shed around us, baring the branches of their saccharine sweetness.

In those hazy mornings that made up our days, I indulged him to escape the maddening boredom that came with being a teenager in Holden. With the exception of an occasional frown from Sol Flores, we went by relatively undisturbed. On the days that I found myself the subject of her scrutiny, I wondered if he noticed her at all: Sol, with her eyes cast towards him in silent dismay. I wondered if he thought about her late at night, before sleep took a hold of him. I wondered if he found her pretty.

One particular morning, I was writing Ezra a note about Lily Abram's unbearable attitude when Mr. Pierre-Louis addressed us for an exercise. "Narnie, Ezra—you guys listening?"

I blushed, covering my post it.

"What I was saying is that I want you all to lock eyes with the person sitting across from you. So Jonah, look at Justin. Adrian, look at Sol. Sally, Nora—and so on and so on. I don't need to teach you all the basics of locking eyes with someone across from you, do I?"

I looked up at Ezra, who was already looking at me.

"He's a little mad, isn't he?" he whispered.

"A little?" I whispered back. "More like absolutely insane."

"Alright everyone, locked?" Mr. Pierre-Louis continued. He opened his battered copy of The Things We Carried as a part of our unit on unconventional existential texts. "While I load our discussion questions, I want you guys to share with each other a quote from the novel that has meaning in your life. A confessional statement, if you may."

Although the classroom often erupted in discussion after his instructions, silence enveloped it this time around like an irrevocable presence. "Seriously, nobody?" he pressed, arching an eyebrow. "Come on, you guys. Give O'Brien some credit. Tell me you all did the damn reading."

After another round of eerie silence, Sol parted her lips to say, "What sticks to memory, often, are those odd little fragments that have no beginning and no end, page thirty six," and when I tilted my head to focus on her sunken eyes, I saw grief. It was the first time I saw her as vulnerable as she did then. My heart ached for her all the same, even though it had no right to.

"Nicely done, Sol," Mr. Pierre-Louis applauded with a smile. "Anyone else?"

On Mr. Pierre-Louis' cue, everyone fragmented into their discussion groups. When I turned around to address our table, Sol laughed nervously. "You guys, that was complete bullshit what I said. I don't even know what the quote means."

Ezra and I exchanged knowing looks, recognizing a lie when we heard one.

She diverted from the topic and began talking about her weekend plans with Adrian, while Ezra flipped to a random page of The Things We Carried, hesitated momentarily, and slipped it over to my end. Confused, I picked it up, eventually seeing that he had highlighted a sentence.

I survived, but it is not a happy ending.

I parted my lips, staring up at him. His expression was innocuous, the usual pursed lips and twinkling eyes, but all I could think about as our gazes became intertwined was how intrigued I was by this boy who was becoming less of a stranger by the day.

I thought about those words incessantly until I was met with his familiar green eyes the following evening during my very first tailgate. The boys were celebrating their triumph against Cedar Lane in their first game of the season. After seven humiliating losses, Ezra had been the one to shatter their dismal streak. Because he was the only change Coach Washington had invested in that season, everyone attributed the victory to him. In a sea of anarchic faces and chaotic chatter, our eyes met before his lips took on a smile.

I blushed, looking away.

"Narnie?" Sol's voice met my ear, anchoring my attention back to my spot on the parking lot.

I met her gaze. "Yeah?"

She took a slight step forward, her anklet ringing quietly. "I know this is a little weird flex, but you and Ezra—is there anything there?"

I pressed my lips together, briefly recalling Lolita Akbar's confession about Sol in the girls' locker room some weeks ago. I wondered if it was mere hearsay or a reason to question Sol's intentions.

"I don't mean to be invasive," she continued. "I just want to respect you in case you two are together."

"Why? Are you interested in him?"

"Asking for a friend," she said softly. "But if she did pursue him, it would be merely out of boredom. So if there's a connection there, she's sensitive to that."

"No connection," I said dismissively. "He's just another boy."

But he was more than just another boy, wasn't he? Why else would he arrive at my doorstep that very evening, the deafening engine of his Harley jolting Nana awake from her evening nap?

He arrived along the curb like a new beginning. Around us, the leaves were beginning to change color, the browning of the hawthorns signaling the evanescence of a sultry summer. He parked his Harley before our driveway. As I observed him through our living room window, I thought back to last summer, to the days of San City, when Papa was still plucking rhubarb leaves from our greenhouse—and on weekends, when he challenged Trevor and I to rounds of badminton on our sidewalk. Mama would watch from the third step of our porch, her eyes deflecting between her laptop and the three of us. Sometimes, when the birdie flew into a treetop, she would laugh as she watched Papa rustle the branches to retrieve it.

I smiled at the memory while Nana rolled over on our reclining sofa. "Don't tell me you're mingling with the delinquents from Port Orion, Narns."

"He's from Holden, Nana."

I tended to the door to find myself standing before his looming frame. As my eyes found his, I inadvertently caught the specks of honey in them. In the leaves of the surrounding sycamores that had yet to change color, I saw the green of his irises. He took one step closer to the doorway—to me. "Narnie, we won."

"I do believe congratulations are in order."

He extended his arms, offering me his helmet. "Celebrate with me?"

I looked down at my polka dotted pajamas. "I should change."

"Why? You look adorable."

I felt my face gather warmth. "Ezra."

He gently pressed the helmet to my stomach. "Come on."

"But Nana," I began.

"Be home by midnight!" she shouted back.

Ezra peeked through the door frame, meeting Nana's gaze. "Pleasure to meet you, Mrs. Larson."

"Of course. Have fun you two. Off with you now," she said, waving us off.

I grabbed his helmet and closed the door behind me. As I clasped it on, he heaved my body over his shoulders. I yelped out his name and he laughed, balancing me on his arms so innocuouslyly that I struggled to contain my heart within my body. I observed him for the fleeting minute that I could, taking in his chiseled jawline, the firmness of his arms and his cheeks, reddened from laughter. Was that because of me?

"Ezra?" I asked once our laughter subsided.

"Yeah?"

"What did you mean that day? You know, when you said you survived, but it wasn't a happy ending."

He placed me down on his Harley. "Maybe I'll get around to telling you one of these days."

We were met with a crisp September breeze as he sat in front of me. I wrapped my arms around him, resting my head on his back. "A story for another time?"

"Yeah, another time."

With that, he took off. We moved at the speed of light until we reached a promenade in the heart of Port Orion bustling with unfamiliar faces. Bodies oppressed by the early September heat crowded the waterfront, the stench of cigar and perfume saturating the atmosphere. In that spacious greenery occupied by sweaty bodies, I saw motorcycles on every corner—Harleys, Ducatis and Yamahas—while their owners enjoyed a drink or two nearby. We parked Ezra's Harley along the lot and made our way toward the crowd. A few meters away, a stage had been set where a local band was performing a dreadful song about nostalgia.

I looked around, taking in my surroundings. What was this place?

"Welcome, Narnie, to the races," Ezra said, as if reading my mind.

"The races? What are the races?"

He pointed to the side of the promenade adjacent to the main road, where two Yamahas were preparing for takeoff.

My eyes widened. "Wait, they're literally racing?"

"Yeah."

"Oh my god. How fast do they usually go?"

"Wouldn't be surprised if they crossed a hundred fifty."

"One hundred fifty miles per hour?"

He nodded.

"What's your record?"

"I don't really race often," he said sheepishly.

"But when you did do it, how fast did you go?"

"Maybe a little over a hundred."

"A hundred? Seriously?"

He led us down a path leading to the water, his lips pressed in a thin line of secrecy. I wanted to ask him so many questions. I wanted to ask him about his Harley and how he had come to own it at just eighteen—and why he had brought me here, out of all places? Was this a glimpse of him or just another one of our many adventures?

"Cute pajamas," an unfamiliar voice met my ears, breaking me from my reverie. A slightly older man with striking eyes approached us. "She's a cute one, Ez. Where'd you find her?"

We ignored him until he stepped in front of us, a beautiful woman draped in his arms. Ezra faltered before her. "What do you want, Alex?"

"A race," he settled. His blue eyes found mine. "What do you say, sweetie?"

Ezra firmly placed his hand on my back, pulling me into him. "Don't talk to her like that."

The woman beside him pouted, running her fingers through her cascading auburn hair.

"Not this time, Larisa," Ezra said softly.

"Please?"

He looked directly ahead, his eyes distant, before asking me for approval. My heart sank to the pit of my stomach at his sudden fragility. Who was Larisa and what did she mean to him—and how did she have the power to make him agree to her in a matter of seconds?

We made our way to the Harleys. When her eyes met mine later that night, she dropped her eyebrows to shade her scowl. I swallowed, wrapping my fingers around the Harley's rear handle.

"Close your eyes," Ezra whispered, leaning backwards.

I closed them.

The races had begun.

CHAPTER 4

In Mr. Chakrabarti's class, we learned that Holden was discovered centuries ago by seafarers escaping exile in Scandinavia. They had established a devout religiosity in the town's constitution that had survived the test of generations. To this day, those born and bred within its twenty square miles trusted its founders' belief in an unquestionable higher power. While a wave of modern secularism had transformed Port Orion and the surrounding villages, Holden had yet to see radical change. That is why Nana slipped into my bedroom the next morning in an effort to awaken me for a trip to the abbey.

"Narnie?"

I moaned, groggily rolling over to the other side of my bed.

"Narnie, hey, wake up," she murmured, shaking me gently. I grunted again, but she continued shaking me, this time with more firmness. "Narns, come on, wake up. We have to go to the abbey. And you have a lot of explaining to do, young lady!" I placed a pillow over my head, her muffled voice nevertheless meeting my ears. "That boy with the motorcycle. When were you planning on telling me about him?"

My eyes snapped open. "Who? Ezra?"

"Have you been seeing this young man—Ezra?"

"Nana," I groaned. "We're just friends. And isn't it Saturday?"

She sat on the corner of my bed. "We have to go to the abbey."

"Abbey?" I asked in disbelief. "What's the abbey?"

"What do you mean what's the abbey? Didn't your parents teach you anything about our religion?"

I stared at her blankly, not knowing what to say.

"The abbey," she began, "is where we pray, Narnie Larson."

"Pray? At seven in the morning?"

"Yes, dear. The sermon starts in an hour so you better get ready."

"Nana—"

"I'll wait downstairs," she said, making her way toward the door.

I parted my lips, wanting to argue that religious sermons were good for nothing but propaganda, but Nana had already left, closing the door behind her. My parents weren't particularly religious. Having renounced their faith at an early age because of their distaste for organized religion, they entertained vaguely spiritual thoughts at most. Mama was originally from Nepal, a Hindu, while Papa had followed the town's religion until he no longer had to. They hadn't entered a religious site since high school. I was a lot like them, preferring spirituality to traditional religion.

I fell back on the bed, snapping my eyes shut for a few more minutes of rest.

"Narnie!" Nana called out, perhaps suspecting that I was going back to sleep.

I sighed, reopening my eyes.

I slipped into Nana's car as the sun rose above suburbia, clad in a soft winter jacket and Mama's favorite woolen scarf. The heat had finally subsided into a chillier consistency. Nana dialed up the radio on our way to the abbey, leading us to ride to nothing but a faint tune and static.

She took the road less traveled, navigating a wraparound and driving us upward. While the abbey was spatially in our town, it was higher in altitude, surrounded by rolling hills and distant white mountaintops, coated in snow. As the sun peeked through the misty hills, we drove up the treacherously narrow roads on top of which the abbey lay.

It was like any other religious sanctuary, but most closely resembled a monastery. I discovered within my first few minutes in its cement walls that the religion was an unconventional hybrid of Islam, Buddhism and Christianity. The congregation hall was adorned in a canopy of golden sculptures from as early as its inception. It led to a lectern behind which the head abbot stood. His name was Edem Whittaker.

Nana murmured a prayer before sitting on one of the wooden benches cascading down the room. I sat next to her as people streamed in through the entryway—Sol, Anderson, Mateo and Isabella—accompanied by their families, until the sermon finally began. The sermon itself passed like most uneventful things do, leaving you with the dread that comes with wasted time. When it was finally time for Nana and I to gather our belongings to leave, the head abbot approached us with an innocuous smile that distinctly resembled Ezra's. "Good morning, Sofia. How are you?"

"Great, thank you, Edem. This is Narnie, my granddaughter."

His eyes wandered to mine. "I thought I identified a new face."

"Pleasure to meet you, Edem."

"The pleasure is all mine, Narnie. You're enjoying Holden so far, I reckon?"

I bit my lip, my thoughts wandering to Ezra.

"I take that as a yes."

"It's lovely," I said. "The people, at least."

"She's met a boy," Nana said sheepishly.

"Nana," I groaned.

Edem chuckled, the gesture meeting his eyes. "How exciting."

"Exciting, but also nerve wracking. You know how young girls are. Is there anything else, Edem? I'm a bit behind on some errands..."

"Actually, Nana, you go," I told her. I looked around the hall at the artifacts. I wanted to explore this place more, to take some pictures outside of the beautiful mountaintops. "I have a question for Edem before heading out."

Her eyes brightened at my sudden interest in the abbot. "Would you mind giving her a lift to town, Edem?"

A small smile graced his chiseled face. He must have been young—in his mid thirties at the latest—and I wondered when he had made the decision to devote his life to a higher power. "Of course, Sof."

Nana kissed my cheek before taking her leave.

I faced Edem as she walked away. "How do you know, Edem?"

"Know?"

"How do you know that your faith is not fiction?"

He recoiled, pleased with my question despite its abrasiveness. "A curious one, aren't you?" When I said nothing, he turned towards the sculptures. "Modern science is good at what it does, Narnie, but it is not enough. It does not account for the immaterial. If you will follow me?"

He led me to a room full of paintings beside the congregation hall, stopping before one in particular. His fingers gently caressed its exquisite frame. According to an inscription, it was carved by Nikolas Oerding, a sixteenth century carpenter with a penchant for metalwork. I examined the painting contained within it, painted by a certain Joannes Parker, its intricate caricatures and colorful violence.

"When you look at this," he began, "tell me, what do you see?"

I looked at it again, taking in the mystical blue of the main subject. A figure resembling a human stood beside him, an axe in hand and in the process of lifting it to kill him.

"I see a person trying to chop off the head of another."

"Can you guess who that figure might be? The one in blue?"

"I'm not sure..."

"It's supposed to represent God."

My eyes hastened toward Edem's. His face was austere as he examined the painting himself. "It's all symbolic, of course. Our belief is that if we wish to achieve any degree of divine awareness, we must first destroy all ideas we have of who God may be. Because you know, if God does exist, they are beyond what we can fathom, as our conception will always be constrained within the finite boundaries of our imagination. So to answer your question, Narnie, this faith is not a fiction because it does not pretend to have answers. It encourages uncertainty—revels in it, even."

Rendered just a little speechless, I glanced at the piece in wonder.

"Is there anything else you'd like to know?"

"Joannes Parker. The painter. Who was he?"

"One of the founders of Holden. Known to be quite the revolutionary."

"And his descendents?"

"I do believe it's a young man by the name of Ezra Parker. I hear the father's in prison. Murdered the mother in cold blood."

I felt my body go numb.

"It may be mere hearsay. We can never tell with things around here."

"Maybe you know better than to spread hearsay, Edem," I said shakily.

He sighed, turning away from the painting. "Thankfully the boy is being taken care of."

"I'm ready to go now, Edem."

He nodded, leading me to his car. I worried for Ezra's wellbeing as I slipped inside. The desire to take pictures had suddenly gone astray.

The smell of rosemary incense flooded the narrow vicinity inside the car. Sitting down, I observed the rearview mirror from which long wooden beads hung. The center of the dashboard was garnished in vermillion.

It took Edem fifteen minutes to pull into our street. Halfway into the journey, a droplet of rain fell before us. Laden clouds billowed in from the east, stifling the voyages of the dragonflies in the nearby horizon. As a cumbersome stillness veiled suburbia, the scent of an oncoming rainfall seeped in through his barely open windows. Just outside, an enthusing silver of lightning flashed in the fleeting way of our lives. With an unsettling bark, the downpour began.

Edem activated his windshield wipers, pulling over along our curb. "I hope I was of some help today, Narnie."

I unbuckled my seatbelt, providing a polite smile. "You were. Thank you."

"Feel free to drop by the abbey if you ever need anything."

I expressed my gratitude one more time before exiting his car. I felt uneasy with him, like I needed to get out of there. Behind me, the door closed with a deafening thud. It was certainly exaggerated by the thunder cleaving in the distance as a bottle of pills fell from his passenger seat all too quickly, dissolving in the water streaming down the gutter.

I picked up the prescription bottle in an effort to save what was left. It was a benzodiazepine used to treat severe insomnia. As I watched Edem drive away, I made a mental note to return it to him the next time I saw him.

Time passed unfailingly every day. I became accustomed to the monotony of suburbia: to the routine and the mundane chaos. Mama buried herself in her work, hiding in her office even during holidays, when Nana and I held a barbeque with the neighbors before the dreadful Holden winter could confine us indoors.

I was absentmindedly browsing through my phone one weekend when Bella ushered me over from her driveway. I looked up from my veranda to hers. "Narnie!" she exclaimed. "Come on, I want to introduce you to my brother, Micah."

Micah never came to the barbeques. Like my mother, he was a notorious workaholic. I had heard about him in Bella's stories: that he was funny, kind and an unfailing optimist. He lifted his hand in a hand in a slight wave.

I smiled, sitting next to him as Bella headed into their kitchen. She had a soft spot for him that her eyes expressed with unequivocal pride. Her love had been strengthened in the past year as Micah had been in San City, completing his law degree. When she came back to the veranda, Micah and I were talking about his distaste for the law. I plopped further myself down on the chair, taking a bottle of lemonade beer from Bella's hand.

"So what brings you to Holden in the middle of the semester, Micah?"

He smiled cheekily, ruffling his baby sister's hair. He looked like her, but more carefree, like he was equipped for any adversity the world had to offer. "Her."

"Seriously, Micah?" she groaned. She shook her head and handed him a beer. "Micah's doing an externship in Holden. Pro bono stuff with his firm. Won't tell us anything about it."

"Client attorney privilege," he said simply.

Bella rolled her eyes. "You're not even an attorney yet."

"Is it too late to change course?"

"Micah!"

"What? It's an absolute pain, going through cases and statutes. And you'd think we get paid for going through the torture."

"You're being paid with experience."

"I guess."

"Why are you doing it then?" I asked him. "I mean, if you hate it so much."

"Because I care about people," he answered, meeting my eye once again. "And because someone I love very deeply may be in danger."

Bella bit her lip. "Elephant in the room much?"

"I don't think he wants to talk about it, Bella."

She rolled her eyes, standing up from her chair. "It'll be a miracle if he opens up about anything. I'm going to go make some tacos. You guys hungry?"

Micah shook his head while I said "No thanks" at the same time.

"Knowing you, you're going to make them anyway," he said in amusement. And he was right. We ended up accompanying her to the kitchen, Micah and I. They were a wonderful team, Micah chopping up the ingredients while Bella fixed tortillas from scratch. As they put the tacos together, I finished what remained of my beer. They were done not much later, Bella pridefully balancing two trays of tacos on her arms. "Voila! Which one do you want, Narnie? There's fried shrimp and there's beans, in case you're a madman like Micah and don't eat meat."

"Haven't sworn off meat yet, but I'll take the beans."

"Good pick," Micah said, handing me a tray of red bean tacos.

I smiled at Micah before digging into my tacos. The day unraveled like most nostalgic days do, with an arresting urgency and fleetingness. Before we knew it, Micah, Bella and I had left their kitchen for greater adventures in Port Orion. Micah drove us to a lakeside to watch the setting sun. As the lakewater lapped behind us, we formed a circle on a patch of nearby grass.

Micah was studying law to become a human rights lawyer. Like my mother, he wanted to devote his life to fighting for the powerless—and Bella was just as much of an idealist, hoping to one day become a developmental economist. She wanted to work in the Congo and stop foreign corporations from harvesting blood minerals for overseas consumption. We were all preoccupied with things bigger than ourselves. That only brought us closer together.

Micah was especially reserved around his baby sister, so she compensated by filling in his silence with her musings. "I feel like I'm trapped in time," she would say.

I did too, in many ways. I was trapped in late August, sobbing violently into my pillow as Mama waited outside my locked bedroom door.

Around us, widely spaced lavender trees formed the perimeter of the lake. The familiar faces of Holden's football team formed clusters around us, chilling their Stellas on the icy water while their friends exploited them for an occasional can or two. The evening was buzzing with conversations when the deafening noise of a motorcycle illuminated the vicinity. I whipped my head sideways—and I saw him.

It was like Bella said. We were suddenly trapped in time.

I followed Ezra's movements as he removed his helmet, revealing his familiar face. His four o' clock shadow was more prominent than it usually was, his lackluster gaze lacking their usual vibrancy. He looked around the promenade, oblivious to the fact that I was observing his dark circles that were not there a few days ago.

Mama would say that when a person intrigues you, you begin to notice the little things about them that you would never notice about anyone else. You begin to search their face for tiny birthmarks, you begin to memorize the color of their eyes and you no longer need to look at them to recite the faint blemishes on their face that even their oldest friends could not recite with confidence. I closed my eyes, easily recalling his soft features: the sharpness of his jaw, the striking green in his glance and the faint dots of birthmarks canvassing his face. When I opened them again, he was still standing there, his eyes on a mission.

Bella cleared her throat. "Narnie?"

I felt my body gather warmth all at once. "Yeah?"

"You want to make it any more clear that you're dying to fuck him?"

"What are you talking about? I just want to be his friend."

Micah raised an eyebrow.

She leaned into me secretively, whispering, "Friends? Seriously? Friends don't undress each other with their eyes."

"I'm not—"

"Hi Narnie."

My breath hitched in my throat.

"I hope I'm not intruding. You were the first person I saw."

If I needed any indication that he felt the same way, maybe this was it. But I fumbled for words, still gravely unassured. Bella filled in the silence once again, smiling warmly at Ezra. "You're not intruding."

"Nice to see you again, Bella."

"You too, Ezra."

Ezra's eyes traveled to Micah. "Ezra," he said, extending a hand.

Micah took it. "Micah. Nice to meet you."

"He's my brother," Bella said sheepishly. "Do you want to sit with us?"

"I'm actually looking for Anderson—Anderson Flemming. Have you seen him?"

Bella's face fell. Beside her, Micah faltered as if the sudden mention of Anderson Flemming resurfaced memories he had long forgotten. He sympathetically glanced at his little sister, who then forced a smile onto her face. "We haven't seen him," she said calmly.

How did Micah know Anderson? I wanted to ask. Instead, I glanced at Ezra. His eyes were already on me, their dullness revealing that he could care less about meeting Anderson Flemming.

"Sleep well?" he asked me.

I nodded. "Like a baby."

"So what are you doing looking for Anderson?" Bella digressed.

Ezra must have sensed Bella's discomfort because he approached the subject with great caution. "Nothing, really. We have some community service hours to make up because Coach Washington caught some boys doing pot in the field." He glanced at her apologetically. "But I'd rather stay with you, Bels. Guy's a bit of a loose end."

The discomfort on her face morphed into a weak smile. "Thanks, Ezra."

"I have to go find him. I guess I'll see everyone another time?"

Bella pretended to glance at her watch. "Actually, Micah and I have to go home as well, run errands for Mom. How long were you going to stay here anyway?"

"Not long—maybe an hour or two."

"Think you can give Narnie a ride home? I'm sure she would much rather stay here."

"Bella!"

Ezra laughed. "What does Narnie want?"

"I," I began. With a simple glance at him, at the way he scavenged my eyes for an answer, I relented. "I'll stay."

Bella and Micah left before we could protest. I don't remember much that came afterwards. All I can remember are my muddled thoughts and weak knees before Ezra Parker, because that was the soft madness life put you through at seventeen, when you were at risk of falling in love for the very first time.

"We don't have to talk about it, but is there a reason Anderson makes Bella completely shut down?" Ezra asked as we watched them walk away. He offered me a hand, which I took to pull myself off the ground.

"Not a clue."

"Is she always like this?'

"I really don't know."

"There's history there, Narns," he said certainly.

"History?"

"Yeah, history. She acts like she's experiencing this awful round of nostalgia over and over again. I remember feeling that way not too long ago. Because it's not just any history, you know? It's the permanent kind. The kind you remember when you're seventy and looking back on life and thinking, what if things hadn't ended the way they did? Would I still be wasting time working my run-down motel in this godforsaken town or would we have made it out? To Mont Blanc or the south of Auckland and not so damn cynical about love." He paused for a moment of silent reflection before meeting my eyes. "You get what I mean?"

"That's a lot to take away from one reaction."

"Maybe. I don't know. You ever have a history like that with anyone?"

I shook my head. No, I didn't...

"Good. You'd get me then. It's like a form of madness. Love is always more cruel the first time around."

I wondered how we had gotten here, to this melancholy discussion about love, and why Ezra had already lost his faith in it at eighteen. I circled my hair in a bun crowning my head, deflecting my eyes from his lips to the park in an attempt to lighten the sombering mood.

"At least there's a possibility for you," I said. "She's still alive, isn't she? And I'm sure certain days don't pass without you glued to her mind. I'm sure she has days when she's stalking your Instagram at three in the morning and tormenting herself over what could have been. But with Papa—" I sighed, abruptly stopping myself.

"What about your Papa, Narnie?"

"I'll see him in the afterlife, if it exists."

A sad smile graced his face. "I suppose you're right. We have our whole lives ahead of us, don't we?"

I wanted to carry on with the conversation—to tell him to let me in so that I could restore his faith in love. But I saw Anderson Flemming waving at us, so I let out a brief "Yeah," and motioned my head toward him. "Speak of the devil."

Ezra followed my eyes, focusing on Anderson. "Come with us?"

I did—and maybe that explained why I was sitting by the lake not much later, observing the boys as they began a game of soccer with the rest of Holden's footballers. I was mindlessly picking the grass, my chaotic thoughts vacillating between homework and university applications when Ezra beckoned the soccer ball in my direction. I caught it between my palms, looking up.

"You any good at soccer?"

I recalled the days not so long ago when Papa and I would circle around Evergreen Park playing soccer with the neighborhood kids. I parted with my melancholy as I stood up to play.

It surprised the boys that I was so good. Unlike San City, girls in Holden seldom played sports. It was too violent—too messy. And girls weren't supposed to dirty themselves around here, not unless they were willing to be stigmatized.

"If our boys had skills like that, our team would actually go somewhere," Nabin, one of the linemen, remarked.

"Seriously, Narnie, you consider anything other than cheerleading?" Aaron Morrison called out. I must have blushed through and through. I did, I wanted to tell Aaron, but it pushed me down a vicious path of memory lane Ezra warned against.

We played until it was just Ezra and I, tossing the ball among ourselves under the violet sky. Night fell upon town, cloaking it with a familiar darkness. We made our way back to Ezra's Harley, the streetlamps paving our way through the jagged pathway.

"I love days like these," he told me. "Days that take unexpected turns and end up being a greater adventure than the adventure you had planned."

My heart swelled in my chest. "Yeah."

"God," he sighed. "I feel so free."

I paused to absorb the beauty surrounding me: the gentle glow of the suburban dusk saturating the green park with Ezra alongside me. These were the days, I thought. These were the days I would be nostalgic for in the long run.

We approached his Harley slowly, knowing that the night was dawning its end without our consent. I reached it before he did.

"You ever drive a motorcycle before, Narnie?"

I looked behind my shoulder, raising an eyebrow at him.

He held up his keys, smiling mischievously. "Do you want to?"

"That's a horrible idea. I'll get us into an accident."

"That's what insurance is for."

"How much does insurance cover though?"

He chuckled a little. "Last chance."

I walked to the edge of his motorcycle, placing my hand on its smooth surface. "I guess I should live a little."

He leaned over my shoulder to insert the key into the ignition. I wondered if he noticed our close proximity as he did that. The heat of his thighs penetrating through my thin corduroy overalls, an unspoken understanding passed between us as I moved my foot to the pedal, gently pushing his away. He leaned over me again, starting the engine.

"Alright, feel the clutch," he said softly.

"Where's the clutch?"

He extended his hands to touch a part of the handles. "There."

I followed my hands to his.

"The clutch is used to change gears. You pull and release it to make sure we don't stall, okay?"

I frowned, finding it difficult to remember his instructions. "Are you sure I can do this?"

"It's easy once you're on the road. Trust me, I wouldn't let you do this if I didn't think you could do it. Just press down with your foot when you're ready. We'll take off easy."

I ignored my hammering heart as I pressed down on the accelerator. The Harley abruptly gathered motion, jolting us forward. "Oh my god."

"You're doing fine, I promise."

He guided me out of the parking lot, intermittently controlling the bike until we looped into the main road. In the post sunset darkness of suburbia, the roads were clear of other cars, so we overran red lights and sped across the silver pavement, taking advantage of the fact that it was just the two of us gliding against this beautiful, cruel world.

"Are we going back home?" I asked him as we passed a green highway sign signaling us toward Holden.

"What do you want?"

"I don't want to."

"Where to then, Narnie Larson?"

"I want to go everywhere. I want to see where you grew up. I want to see your parents' house, your favorite park[illegible], your elementary school—I want to see everything."

"I grew up on the outskirts, Narnie. By the hills of the abbey. 7 Scarpetta Lane."

"I was there this Saturday! And Nana took me to meet Edem. Do you know him?"

His body tensed for the little while that he allowed it to. "Oh, yeah."

"You okay?"

"We have some weird ancestral ties," he explained quickly. I sensed a newfound caution in his voice, subtle but indisputable. If I was any less attuned to his tendencies, it would have passed me by. I brought the Harley to a stop.

"Why are we stopping?" he asked.

I circled around to meet his eye. "Is there something you're not telling me?"

He hesitated, his eyes becoming distant. "I don't have a very fond opinion of the abbot. Mom and Dad always spoke badly of him."

I thought about the pills. I thought about telling Ezra.

"Now is there something you're not telling me?" he said, lifting my chin with his hand.

"The other day when Nana introduced me to him, she left early for work. And somehow Edem ended up dropping me home."

"You were alone with him?"

"Yeah. And he had like, pills in his car. It was a benzodiazepine."

"Benzodiazepine?"

"It's a type of drug used to induce sleep in chronic insomniacs. That's what the label said."

"So the abbot is an insomniac," Ezra said with such a nonchalance that I wondered who he was trying to fool: me or himself.

"I don't know, Ezra. I don't think it's just insomnia. The guy, he gives me the creeps."

"Don't dig into this, Narnie. We have no reason to."

"We talked about you too. He told me about your dad—about what he did. I'm so sorry, Ezra."

His chin slightly trembled.

"Your dad—is he really in prison?"

A moment of silence passed between us. "He is," he finally said. "But not for reasons you would think. Can we maybe talk about this some other time?"

I nodded, ignoring the sudden edge in his voice. The traffic of passersby grew as I drove us back to the village. And I had hoped that our goodbye would not be as short—as callous—but Ezra was brief as he dropped me outside our house, asking me if he could take it from there. And when I saw him again the morning after in Mr. Pierre-Louis' classroom, he pretended last night never happened.

"Hey," he said briskly. There was no follow up the way there often was: no banter, whispers or sticky notes taped onto my desk. So I began guarding myself. I became less receptive to his cues and began avoiding him out of fear of loss.

It was not like Ezra was trailing behind me, craving my attention anyway. He occupied himself with his books that he knew best. In those moments lost in translation between us, I treated cheerleading like an extreme sport. There were seldom shy glances the way there used to be. We went from potentially being something to strangers all at once.

"I'm still convinced he likes you," Bella said over lunch a few days later, sprinkling her fries with salt and pepper. "I mean, come on, the guy gave you his jacket."

"But that was weeks ago, Bels. He was just being nice."

"Ezra? Nice?" she asked, arching an eyebrow. "I thought he was an ass."

"He is."

"Then?"

I pressed my lips together, eyeing my noodles that were going cold. "It's complicated."

Bella casted her eyes downward, shaking her head in disapproval. "Honestly? Take my advice, Narnie. Run far away from complication. Zen. Be a monk."

I smiled at her. "As you say, Isabella."

The days carried on without my permission, September dissipating into a chilly October that forced me out of my long sleeved dresses into sweaters and heavy jackets. The beginning of autumn went on uneventfully with Ezra's seat empty in Existential Literature. I became starved of his presence as silence overcame the room when Mr. Pierre-Louis called his name. "Ezra Parker," he would say, often repeating his name in between silences as if it would make him reappear.

Whenever he was there, he made his presence known to the best of us. With his passionate political commentary and existential remarks at eight in the morning, I wondered how one person could carry within them such fire, one never at risk of burning out.

One day when we were exchanging our copies of The Things We Carried to decode one another's annotations, he tossed his battered copy marked at page 38 to me. He had highlighted a quote which read, We steadily increase our moral capital in preparation for that day when the account must be drawn down.

"What about it, Ezra?" I asked angrily. I was upset with him for ending our friendship so abruptly.

"What do you make of that quote?" he asked, his eyes boring into mine.

My eyes bled into the paper, preempting a hollow silence.

He sighed. "Turn to page 58."

I survived, it read, but it was not a happy ending.

"You've showed me this before."

"Do you see the relationship between the two?" he asked. When I said nothing and merely continued gawking at the pages of the novel, he dropped his elbows on the desk before him. "Listen, Narns. This guy, he fears death. He fears it so much he thinks it's the worst thing in the world."

"But he's right. Death is the worst thing in the world."

"He changes."

"Changes how?"

"He ends up saying he survived, but it was not a happy ending. O'Brien is emphasizing something there, you know? A really important point." He paused, looking at me for a sign of understanding. When I offered nothing, the look in his face indicated that he was done with me forever. "Narnie," he implored, his voice softening. "Come on, don't you get it? He's saying that there are certain things in life worse than death."

"Like what, Ezra?" I asked, looking away. "What can possibly be worse than death?"

"You know what. If there's anybody I trust to know that, it's you."

"Well, I don't know it."

"It's this grief," he finally said. "That's what's worse than death."

With that, the bell rang, signaling the end of class. As he raced to the next hour, a tiny slip of paper fell from his copy of The Things We Carried. By the time I could pick it up, he had already left—and when I read its contents at last, I sided against my better judgement and kept it for myself. It was a poem, a poem he had written for his pretty eyed lady:

i met her in my glory days
when i was chasing dreams, getting high,
and fighting heinous demons by the sunrise;
kaleidoscopic visions and dull sensations,
pursuing petty ambitions,
wasted by the water, there she lay,
pretty eyed lady, there you lay,
you, with your torturous elegance,
my heart beating for your body's wake;
you weaved me stories of seduction and ruse;
oh pretty eyed lady, a sinner, my muse;
you puckered your lips for show,
watched my infatuation grow,
pretty eyed lady, who could not admire you?
with the way your body wept
in pain, as you kept
your convictions unknown;
oh pretty lady, your irises brimming with adventure,
how your presence still lingers,
how you had the stars wrapped around your fingers;

and while you suppressed the galaxies burning inside of you,
deflamed your passion and let sadness desensitize you,
your breath strokes birthed constellations on my skin;
pretty eyed lady, you comforted me with sin,
watched me light a joint in your grace,
precarious high wires all around;
we set houses on fire with our passion,
bed sheets were set ablaze by tender motions;
pretty eyed lady, i waited for you after that night
when you told me that i do not know love,
and that all I am is fire,
a wicked flame consumed by a penchant for desire,
and that, indeed, you crave someone better
a someone who is gentler;
and the planet encircled in its sporadic orbits,
for thirteen months, we missed sunsets and traipsed through
the ashy remnants of the houses we burned down;
now you are the only home that remains intact;
so what of it now, pretty eyed lady?
tell me now before it is too late,
how wrong am i in still loving you;
how much longer will i have to wait?

I lay in bed, reading it over and over again until it made my insides hollow. I read it during the fleeting breaks in between classes, indulging my depressed fantasies about his pretty eyed lady. I read it pretending I could mean something to him.

After the guilt of keeping it wore away, I began using it as a bookmark. And when I did see him in those minutes of translation in and out of classes, I avoided him out of remorse, wondering if he ever looked for it—if he even found it missing.

I spent my afternoons with Micah. After cheerleading practice, when Bella was volunteering in Fort Montgomery and Nana shopping in the village, he would rock away on a wooden chair on their veranda, always in a suit, ready for work. The utmost button of his dress shirt unbuttoned and his collars popped, he sat with a laptop barely balanced on one knee and a legal pad on the other; and he carried two pens: one tucked behind his ear and another on his hand, which he used to write with.

I remember driving home one evening to find him sitting on the front steps, not in formal attire but in a pair of ripped jeans and a hoodie. He toyed with an unfinished bottle of beer as he stared into the distance, his eyes marked in enigma.

I dropped my backpack beside him. "Done for the day, Micah?"

He lifted his head toward me, a weak smile gracing his chiseled face. "Hey, Narnie."

"You okay? You look like death."

He was quiet for the longest time. I pulled his arm, occupying the empty space next to him. "Micah, hey."

"Sorry. I'm just feeling very defeated."

"What's the matter?"

"Thinking about relationships that never happened," he said. "It's dumb."

"Who is she? Did you leave her behind in San City?"

He chuckled, taking a sip of his beer. "It wouldn't be as tragic if I had."

"Come on, Micah. I never pegged you for a pessimist."

"It's just a very hard thing to wrap my head around. Like, if two people love each other very deeply, why does shit force them apart?"

"What kind of shit?"

"I don't know—complicated stuff. I'm sorry. I don't mean to be so cryptic about all of this. It's just, being in this town and seeing you with Bella reminds me of her."

"I understand."

We lapsed into another silence.

I sighed. "Hey, Micah?"

"Yeah?"

"I don't mean to nauseate you with my optimism, but you know that greek mythology? The one Plato brought into our collective awareness some years ago before his death. He claimed that we were originally born with four arms, four legs and a head with two faces, and that Zeus, fearing our capability, split us into two entities, sentencing us to spend our miserable lives in search of our other half. This idea of soulmates—of a connection so rare and divine that it can never be severed—don't you believe in it, Micah?"

"I can't help but feel like those are the words of someone who has never been in love."

"You think Plato never fell in love?"

"Plato never addresses the pain you encounter in the quest to find your one true love. In his idealistic theory, he does not consider the melancholy."

"But—"

"I get it, Narnie. I get that there are people out there who fuck at forty even after denying it for decades. But there are also people out there who are pulled apart by fate, every single day, for no obvious reason. Does their love have less value because they didn't make it?"

I recoiled, shrinking into my seat. "It's not supposed to come easy, you know. It seems like you're fighting the shitty things anyway, if you did come back for her."

"Yeah."

Micah was discreet about many things, but it became clearer throughout the days that he hadn't just come back for the greater good. He had come back for love.

With Micah, I fell on a schedule, completing my homework as he worked on his many assignments—and when he wasn't with me, he was with Mama, collaborating in her office as the gentle hum of their voices droned faintly within its soundproof walls.

I focused on myself more, throwing myself into extracurricular activities and university applications. And I accompanied Nana on her visits to the abbey more often, taking my time to explore its cryptic rooms while waiting for her to finish her prayers. Its architecture often took me back to the Renaissance: bronze chandeliers in every room, intricate woodwork along the high ceilings and old furniture meticulously placed on every corner, with detailed carvings, velvet fabric and clawed feet.

Visitors to the abbey were confined within the space around the main hall and advised not to wander, but my curiosity often led me astray. On one particular morning, I denied my better judgement and walked along the main corridors to a pair of spiraling staircases. I took the road less travelled down the stairs, admiring the artwork lining the walls despite their eerie historical undertones.

The steps led to a library built entirely on mahogany. Its perimeter clad in books, there was nothing else but a desk containing a lamp, rusty books and dilapidated photographs of former abbeys throughout their pilgrimages. I walked along the library, caressing the binds of the books, until my eyes found Siddhartha.

My heart swelled with the thought of Ezra as I took it out. I opened the book, coughing up the dust that had gathered over the years. Before I could flip through its pages, my eyes spotted

Clara Parker along its edge. I arched an eyebrow. Parker? Like Ezra Parker?

I placed the book back on the shelf and took out another, a *South of the Border, West of the Sun* by Haruki Murakami. Sienna Flores was written along its edge this time around. I could feel my heart hammering in my chest as I put it back, the benzodiazepine fresh in my mind. I considered for the first time in my life that I was somewhere I should not have been—that I was in danger.

I ran up the steps just as quickly as I had arrived. Down the corridor on my way back to the hall, I was met with Edem's curious face. A moment of fear crossed his eyes.

"Narnie! Sweetie, we were looking for you," Nana said.

I slid into my sweater, breathing nimbly into the air. "Just admiring the paintings."

"Not to worry, dear. Ready to go?"

I nodded, crossing over to Nana. We quietly made our way toward the doorway, Edem trailing behind us.

"Enjoy the paintings?" he asked me, his voice somehow more sharp—more cunning.

"Yeah," I said, feigning a smile. "Great collection, Edem."

"Time to go now, Narns," Nana ushered. She waved at Edem. "Until next time, Edem."

He nodded, stepping backwards. "Have a great week, Sofia."

We found Nana's car with relative ease. As we slipped inside, I nudged her. "Hey Nana, do you know anyone named Sienna Flores?"

"Sienna Flores, now that's a name I haven't heard in a while."

"Is she at all related to Sol Flores?"

"Why, she's Sol's twin sister!"

"And Clara Parker?"

Nana froze. "What about Clara Parker?"

"Do you know her?"

"Both of these girls went missing sometime ago, dear. Poor things. Clara is believed to be dead. The Parkers left shortly after the coroner's ruling, but their young one—Ezra, is that his name? The boy you're always with. It seems he's back in town."

Ezra had a sister? I remembered that he did. He had mentioned her in passing.

"I don't know who's looking after that boy these days, but the Parkers always sheltered him. After what happened to Clara, they sent him off far away from Holden."

And now he was back. But why?

I felt a distinct restlessness to talk to him. Even though we were strangers now, I wanted to tell him what I saw; I wanted to tell him that maybe there was more to Edem than meets the eye.

"What's sparked your curiosity all of a sudden?"

"Just heard some people talking about them in school," I said casually, but my hands began to shake, giving me away. I was relieved to see that Nana was too focused on driving to notice.

"The town is prone to a lot of gossip, but many say the girls are still out there."

"Has anyone seen them?"

"I don't know, dear. I don't think so. And with the disappearances that have been happening lately, I'm worried things are taking a turn for the worse again."

I slid deeper into my sweater, looking out the window as we descended unto the village. When I was finally home, I locked myself in my bedroom and pondered the excuses I had to talk to Ezra again. And the days turned into nights, long nights into shorter days, but we didn't turn into anything more.

Chapter 5

Misfortunes continued.

Rumors exploded like wildfire that the serial killer was on his fifth victim. Muddled videos of passersby setting fire to political caricatures plagued local news. Nana would sit in front of our television, knitting away at a sweater while News 8 looped clips for its hungry audience.

"Hey, did you hear?" Bella said one morning on our way to school. "Apparently the latest victim is a student in school. All the parents are losing their shits. They don't know if it's safe for us to even be in school."

I understood the outrage. It was the kind of thing my parents would lose their shit over. I don't know why but it reminded me of a silly memory of Mama and I, from when I was sixteen. Unlawful searches are a violation of your constitutional rights, Mama would say, her voice mischievous with a hint of seriousness. Here's a pocket constitution if you ever see your rights being taken advantage of, baby.

"Mom!" I groaned, looking away. I was almost late for my date with Harrison Cooper, my first date and every other teenage girl's dream. "Harry's got better things to do than violate my constitutional rights."

"You never know when you'll need it," she said, winking at me. "Your father has taught me that boys can be vicious, as a matter of fact."

"I'm not carrying that around with me!"

"Narnie!"

"Mom," I groaned, plopping myself on the couch. I pulled my socks from aside, hastily sliding into them.

She pressed her lips together in disapproval. "So you won't take it?"

I shook my head, rushing to Mama's side and dropping a kiss on her cheek. "Keep your phone close. I'll call you if I need to take a case to the Supreme Court, okay?"

"Narnie," Bella groaned, snapping me out of my memory. "I heard they're already calling in suspects. They can literally call in anyone."

"What are you so worried about?"

"I don't know."

"Well, since you literally have no connection to the crime—" Bella's eyes shifted. "—unless," I continued. "You do?"

"It's just, Micah's sensitive about the whole thing. It makes me wonder if that's the reason he came back here. And if that's the case, maybe we'll be the next victims."

"I don't think we need to worry, Bella."

"Maybe we don't. But it doesn't change the fact that I'm still worried. And Anderson keeps looking at me in class. He never does that. He's been really good at staying cruel since we called it quits. So what does it mean that he's suddenly giving me attention?"

"Have you tried talking to him?"

"No."

"I can't tell you what's on his mind, babe."

"I know. I just—sometimes I wonder if I still have feelings for him."

I felt my eyes widen. "You're into Anderson? Anderson Flemming?"

"I know, I know. It's just—"

"You can do so much better, Bella."

"I know—"

"Do you?"

"Ugh, Narnie. You're so annoying. Stop with the commentary and focus on driving."

I brought my eyes back to the road. "Okay, okay, continue."

"Before his girlfriend, Sienna, went missing," Bella began. "Back when we were still on speaking terms. Back when we were friends. I thought we had something special."

"Who was it who told me to stay away from complication?"

"Anderson's not that b—"

"Don't even finish that sentence. Come on, Bella. He'll fuck everything that walks. You know better."

Her shoulders surrendered themselves to dismay. "Now I do," she murmured. I realized then that her feelings were still there—that Ezra had been right that day. There was a history there.

"Did something happen recently?"

"I met up with him in July," she told me in embarrassment. "We kind of—fucked. Okay, don't give me that look. It was like, as a one final hurrah kind of thing."

I stifled a laugh.

Bella sighed. "Let it out."

"What the hell is a one final hurrah kind of thing?" I asked, laughing.

"It was so overdue. I knew he was only with Sienna because it was what his family had wanted for him. When she went missing, he was so miserable and hurting that I gave in to my stupid feelings and approached him. He was resistant then, but then we had this event in July where we got to talking about it again. And it was so intense that we just—did it."

"Jesus."

"And it was really good, the sex."

"Did it ever happen again?"

"We have been doing it ever since."

I turned my head over to her, completely horrified.

"Gee, I'm just joking. No need to get so uptight."

"I'm just looking out for you," I said. I swerved into the road that led us to school. "Do you believe in God?"

She faltered as if I had taken her by surprise. "Yes, I do. Do you?"

"No."

"Why?"

"Well, nobody can prove its existence."

She shrugged, as if she was accustomed to hearing something like that. "Come on, Narnie," she finally said. "Do you really believe that? I think about this sometimes and every time I do I reach the conclusion that the universe is too beautiful to have been an accident."

But the universe was just as cruel as it was beautiful. Because later that week, Sienna Flores returned to town for good. We discovered that she was never missing. She had purposefully left without a trace so as to not be found. The townsfolk hungrily devoured stories about why she had returned now after the long year away.

To celebrate her other half's return, Sol gathered their closest friends and acquaintances in an abandoned railroad station. By a mistake in calculation, she invited me as well, arriving sharply at eight in Nana's driveway to pick me up. With Mateo on her passenger seat, I was wedged between Anderson Flemming and Sienna in the back.

The tracks were surrounded by tall, cascading trees that formed a tunnel of lush foliage until the end of the horizon. Sol parked her pickup truck at the end of the path and led us to the crowd. When we arrived, I was met with the strong smell of mixed drinks and afterrain.

"Welcome back!" everyone shouted as we walked over with Sienna. Among the hundred blurry faces, I looked for Ezra Parker.

"You want a drink, Narnie?" Anderson asked, snapping me out of my reverie.

I looked at him, nodding. "Sure."

He returned less than a minute later with a bottle of Fireball in his hand. "So we have this tradition," he said, "that whenever something wild happens in our lives, we drink Fireball."

I laughed a little. "Who's we?"

"Sol, Mateo, Sienna, Be—and me."

I raised an eyebrow.

"You in?"

I nodded. He led me back to Sol's pickup truck, where they had already set everything up. Sol was two shots into our drinking game when she declared, "I'm going to text him" and Sienna and Anderson both shouted, "No!"

Her eyes flooded with tears. "But I want to."

"I thought you'd deleted his number, bub," Mateo said.

"She has that shit memorized," Sienna said, rolling her eyes.

"I miss him," Sol said in her defense.

"Who?" I asked.

"M—"

"Sol, shut your mouth," Anderson warned.

Sol glared at him. "You shut up, Anderson. So what if I want to tell Narnie?"

"Why don't you tell Narnie in the morning, love?" Mateo offered. "You know, when you're sober."

"But Mateo—"

"Can we continue the game?" Sienna said. "I don't feel anything."

We were all on the back of Sol's pickup truck playing Sevens, a stupid drinking game Anderson had suggested. We couldn't say the number seven, its variations or its multiples. If we did, we had to take a sip of our drink.

"One," Mateo began.

Sol lifted her head from her phone. "Two."

"Three," Anderson said, looking at Sienna.

She rolled her eyes. "Four."

I found four pairs of eyes landing on me. "Five," I said.

"Six," Mateo continued.

"Eight!"

"Nine."

"Ten."

"Eleven."

"Twelve."

"Thirteen."

"Four—Fifteen!"

Anderson filled Sienna's glass with a shot of Fireball. "Drink, Princess."

"For fuck's sake, Anderson," Sienna said with a laugh. She took her shot quickly.

We played for another hour until we had finished two bottles of Fireball and a Moscato. We were at the time of night when everyone was jumping in and out of conversations, the kinds that came from years of uninterrupted history. I leaned against the wall of the truck, absorbing the constellations above me. The night was so beautiful. And I suddenly wanted to dance.

"You know, Sol, if you want to text him, text him. Life's way too short to hold back," I said.

Anderson, Sienna, and Sol turned their heads toward me. Mateo sipped his water, slightly frowning.

"He's a good guy, bub," Sienna said. Her drunk mind was kinder to this stranger, whoever he was. "But he won't be here for long. You know that."

Anderson was far more callous. "No, no and no. He chose to leave you, remember? Don't listen to Sienna. She's out of her mind."

Sol looked down at her lap. "I guess."

Mateo bit his lip, observing the three.

"You're too good for him," Anderson added softly.

"Mateo?" Sol murmured. "What do you think I should do?"

He took another sip of his water, his face containing a hint of melancholy. "You should do what makes you happy, Sol," he said with a weak smile. His eyes twinkled ever so slightly. Maybe I saw in them the reflection of the stars or his longing contained in a way that was careful to not give itself away. "And if it means we have to go through the past all over again, we will. I'm always here for you. You know that."

The night unfolded as many nights do, warm despite the near freezing temperature, with Anderson's cinnamon whiskey and cherry wine strong in my system. When the clock struck ten, I wondered if Ezra Parker was still somewhere here, lost among the crowd. Why I wasted so much of my time thinking about him I did not know—but I knew that I missed him. I missed his Harley and his unpredictable musings about love and loss.

At ten, Sienna was already sprawled on top of Anderson, fast asleep, while he made circles on her wrist. With Mateo and Sol subsumed in a conversation of their own, it was my cue to leave. A dreadful party song began to play as I left the four of them on the back of the truck.

The traffic of people had doubled from before, making it difficult to move comfortably. I navigated the crowd without knowing where I was going, my head spinning from the alcohol.

"Didn't think I'd see you again," a vaguely familiar voice murmured in my ear, spinning me by the waist.

I let my inebriated mind register his features, the sharp jaw and dark hair, thinking back to the early autumn night when Ezra had taken me to the races for the first time.

"Alex," he reminded me. "Remember?"

"I remember," I said—and I did. I remembered the look on Ezra's face as Alex approached us that night, guarded and controlled, like they shared an unwanted history he himself could not atone.

I saw him then. He was standing by the bar, observing us while drinking a Guinness. Our eyes crossed for a fleeting moment before he quickly deflected his gaze from mine, fixing it on someone else▯—on Larisa, who was fixing him a drink. I looked away as well, pretending that seeing him with her didn't make my heartstrings constrict.

"Isn't that your girlfriend, Alex?" I said coldly.

He placed his hands on my hips. "And what about you? Are you Ezra's girl?"

If only.

"You have that look on your face that says that maybe you are."

I looked behind Alex, finding Ezra exactly where he was. Without warning, he swooped Larisa into a dance. I curled my lips at the two of them, at their sudden closeness, as she whispered something into his ear, to which he laughed quietly.

"I'm no one to him."

An amused gleam overcame his eyes. "It's spectacular how wrong you are."

"How would you know? I doubt Ezra's spending his days confiding in you."

His hands faltered behind me. "It's just—it's been a long time since I've seen someone by his side, especially a girl."

I bit my lip, saying nothing.

He gently grabbed my fingers, pulling me into him. "You never told me your name."

"Alex..."

"It's Narnie, right? I could've sworn I heard him call out to you that night."

"What night?" I asked hesitantly.

"After the race. When you two won."

I looked behind him at the two again, feeling my chest constrict again at the sight.

"They're just friends, Narnie."

Were they?

Alex twirled me around. "And I'm sure if you dance with me for long enough, Ezra's gonna come out here trying to be your knight in shining armor."

"Really?"

"You want to find out?"

He didn't wait for an answer as he pulled me into him. I was surprised to discover that he was right—that despite their hostile relationship, he did know Ezra after all. It was only a matter of time before Ezra approached us.

Alex dropped his hands from my waist, a mischievous smile gracing his face. "See?"

"Narnie, what are you doing with him?" Ezra asked me quietly. "Don't you know he's trouble?"

"Alex isn't trouble."

"How do you know who he is?"

"Well, you haven't talked to me in nearly two weeks," I said in my defense. "You're past the stage of dictating who I speak to, don't you think?"

Ezra sighed again, his eyes drooping as if he hadn't slept in days. I wanted to transform into a refuge and offer myself to him. When he spoke at last, he slipped beside me first. "Larisa's just an old friend," he said. It sounded rehearsed, like a script he had been practicing for days, and uttering it aloud gave away his fraudulence.

She appeared before us then, his pretty eyed lady. "Getting into trouble again boys?"

His eyes wandered to her light brown ones. There was something in the way he looked at her, his eyes laced with love, remorse and just a hint of pride.

Alex pulled her into him, planting a fleeting kiss on her forehead. "Hey, Lar."

"Shall we go, Narnie?" Ezra asked me softly.

"Go?" Larisa asked, her eyes widening. "Come on, Ezra, how come you're always leaving so quickly? Whenever I appear you seem to want to vanish."

I squeezed myself closer to him. "I have a curfew."

"A curfew? Seriously? What are we, five?"

"Let's go Ezra," I said, dismissing her.

He gave me a brief nod. And we left. As we approached Sol's pickup truck, he nudged my shoulder. "Hey, Narn," he said shyly—hesitatingly. "If I didn't know any better, I would think you liked me."

I stopped dead in my tracks, spinning to face him.

"I'm flattered, actually," he went on. "It's actually kind of cute that you like me."

He seemed amused, like I was right where he wanted me. I knew from the way our story was going that he would never consider falling in love with me, that I was just another passing thought to him. He was too deeply entrenched in his nostalgic love affair with his first love. I contemplated the likelihood of this story ending for the two of us, but dismissed it just as quickly. After all, characters like me were disposable; we were merely catalysts in the plotplay of cynical authors to prove their bitter points about love and loss.

I scowled, facing him through my indignation. And there he was, standing merely inches away, his eyes twinkling in amusement. I gave him a frustrated shove, my hands shaking with each move. "Get that smug look off your face," I said, hitting his chest with each word. I was so drunk that I was on the verge of tears. "You ignore me for weeks. And now you're out here acting like nothing happened, like we're friends."

He took a step toward me, his face softening. "Narn—"

"Did I say something that night, Ezra? Did I scare you off?"

"No, I just—"

"You just what?"

He was quiet for the longest time. I wondered what it took for him to open up at last. "I didn't like how close we were getting. And it was so easy with you. It happened in a few days. And I thought about what happened to my mom and Clara and I told myself that I couldn't be vulnerable again, not after Clara."

I softened as well, recalling Nana's words from not too long ago about the missing girls. "Clara?"

"My sister, Clara, who disappeared last August. And then you mentioned the benzodiazepine. It caught me off guard. It made me wonder if you were in danger."

"Don't tell me I was right about Edem."

He sighed. "Did you ever talk to him about his insomnia?"

"No," I began. I looked down at my feet, thinking back to the eerie room in the abbey where I had almost been caught.

"What else do you know, Narns?"

"I—I saw a room," I told him, catching his eye. "In the abbey. I wanted to show you."

He pulled his keys out of his pocket. "Let's?"

"Are you crazy? Not in your Harley. It's way too loud."

"How else are we going to get there?"

"I don't know."

He looked away, entrenched in a deep thought. A distasteful feeling arose in the pit of my stomach.

"Narnie?"

"Yeah?"

"They didn't just find her that night, you know. They found her gagged and abandoned, with traces of some benzodiazepine in her system."

"Clara?"

"My mom."

My knees trembled. "You don't think—"

"I don't know."

"Oh my god."

He sighed, gripping his pockets as if he would shrink away. I waited for him to say something—anything—but he squeezed his eyes shut, releasing another sigh. "I'm scared," he finally said, but he did it so quietly that I wondered if he said it at all.

I wondered if we knew who we were up against then—if we knew it when we snuck into the abbey later that night, with nothing but the light of our phones guiding us along the corridors. I could hear Ezra's softly beating heart from just centimeters away.

The room was the same as I had left it, just as velvety and polished, the books untouched. If the lights weren't on, I would wonder if anyone came here at all. I bit my lip, scavenging the spines amid Edem's labyrinth of books for Siddhartha. I was just pulling it from the wall when somebody yanked me into a dark corner, clamping my mouth shut.

My heart sunk to the pit of my stomach at the sudden gesture. I couldn't see the stranger under the cover of darkness, but I could, quite intensely, feel him, like the way his breath tickled my face like a gentle breeze, the way our noses nuzzled due to our close proximity and the way his thighs gently brushed against mine, confining me to that enclosed space. He held me closely until the lights flickered off in the library. When we exited the shadows, I sighed in relief. Ezra.

His face showed no emotion as I motioned toward the copy of Siddhartha on my hand. My heart hammering inside my chest, I showed him the fore edge, where Clara's name was written in cursive.

"That was her favorite book," he said quietly. We took it back with us to Nana's.

I had missed him. I didn't realize just how much until we were back on his Harley, gliding across Holden's unfamiliarly familiar silver streets. I don't know why. It had only been weeks.

We arrived home just before midnight. He must have spent the night rereading that book, over and over again, looking for just one indication that Clara was not gone after all. I fell asleep with my head tucked into his neck. And when I woke up the next morning, he was gone.

CHAPTER 6

Bella drove us to school that morning. She needed the practice. As we breezed through the familiar road, I tried to forget that my life was slowly descending into chaos.

We grabbed breakfast at a nearby coffee shop before heading to our eight a.m. class. I found myself once again in Mr. Pierre-Louis' classroom, surrounded by chatter but in a palpably silent room, with the seat across from mine empty. I listened to him call Ezra's name into an empty air.

I rested my chin on my palms, observing the dry, wintry morning through the window. As I looked at the baring orchards, I found my head racing with endless thoughts. Where could he be? Especially after last night—was he in danger? Had Edem found out about us sneaking into the abbey somehow? My stomach was in knots for the entire hour.

When class finally ended, I took the back door to exit the school. I may have been insane as I got in my car and set the navigator to 7 Scarpetta Lane. My hands shaking against the cold leather of the steering wheel, I braced myself for a thirty minute drive ahead. It took me forty two—I counted.

I walked up the Parkers' property slowly, wondering how I had mustered the courage to come this far. Was I ready for what awaited me ahead? I don't know. All I know is that my blood went cold when Edem's brooding figure greeted me on the other side of the front door. "Narnie," he said, raising his eyebrows. "I wasn't expecting you."

I took an involuntary step backwards. Survival instinct, I suppose. Because out of all the things I was expecting that morning, I wasn't expecting Edem Whittaker to greet me at the door.

"What's going on, dear?" he pressed. "You look like you've seen a ghost."

"I—I'm collecting census data," I fumbled. "Is anyone home?"

"I am. How can I help?"

"You mean this is your home?"

"You didn't know?"

Loosening my scarf on my neck, I met his eye. His focused gaze sent shivers down my spine.

"Would you like to come in?" he asked, opening the door wider for me to enter.

I felt my breathing labor.

"Narnie," he continued, when I didn't answer. "Are you sure you're okay?"

"I'm fine," I managed to say. I needed to get out of there. "I should actually move on. I'm sorry."

"Didn't you have to collect some information?"

"I'm not feeling too well all of a sudden...I should go."

"Are you sure?" he asked in genuine concern. He was an effortlessly charming man—and that terrified me even more. I tried to overlook his hospitality as I nodded my head and walked back to my car.

He left for the abbey not much later. As his car made the steep ascent to the top of the hill, I slipped into his house through a slightly open back window. I must have been in there for hours, looking for a sign to lead me to the end of this mystery. I checked every room in the house, unsure of what I was looking for and finding myself at a loss every time.

I left two hours later when I heard footsteps approaching the front door. As I snuck back into my car, I was surprised to find Micah waiting by its mahogany frame, his fingers reaching for the doorbell ever so often. Clad in a suit, he waited, his feet tapping the wooden veranda atop which he stood.

On the drive back to school, I wondered what Micah was doing there. And I thought about Ezra—about why he had lied about living in 7 Scarpetta Lane? Did he feel like an outcast for not having a home? Did he feel like an outcast even in front of me? I turned on the radio to distract myself from my thoughts, chastising myself for believing I could have meant something to him. If he was a mystery to the rest of Holden, why would I be any different? What reason did he have to let me in?

I pulled into school just in time for lunch. I was opening my locker in search of my lunch box when Sol approached the one beside mine. She opened her door, tentatively glancing at me. "You okay, Narnie? You were there in Allen's eight a.m. but not in calculus."

I forced a smile onto my face, slightly endeared that she had noticed. "I'm okay. Thanks for noticing."

"Of course."

I fumbled for my lunch box, which was suddenly nowhere to be found.

"Hey Sol?"

Her eyes snapped toward me. "Yeah?"

"You haven't seen Ezra today, have you?"

She closed her locker, facing me. Her eyes twinkled as she motioned that I turn around. When I did, I found the devil himself standing there, his footsteps drawing closer with my every breath. I rolled my eyes, slamming my locker door shut. Less than a foot away, Ezra arched an eyebrow. "Heading to lunch?"

"Yeah," Sol said and I said "Like you'd care" at the same time.

He narrowed his eyes at me. "What's the matter?"

I smiled warmly at Sol before walking past him.

"Narnie," Ezra said, trailing after me. But I had already decided that I would never forgive him. Except I would in a heartbeat. "Narns, what did I do?" he asked softly—pathetically.

I ignored him, walking past the cafeteria and main offices, my mind set on nowhere in particular. He finally grabbed my wrist, spinning me around and into the lockers. "Why won't you talk to me?" he pressed, his face suffused with an urgency that I had never seen in him before. Around us, people began to scatter. But how could I tell him what I had done without being vulnerable—without implying that I was very deeply beginning to care about him, that I already did?

When I refused to answer, he gently caressed my chin, forcing me to look at him. "Hey, don't be like this. Come on."

I felt my mouth go dry. Suddenly every word I ever knew vanished from my memory. "Why did you lie to me about where you live?" I asked finally.

His eyes widened.

"I didn't see you in class this morning and I—I didn't know what to do."

"Did Edem see you?"

"You knew? You knew he lived there and you still gave me that address?"

He let go of my wrist, fear veneering his eyes as it often did at the mention of Edem, but today, it was without restraint. It was clearer. "That was our house before Mom was murdered."

"Don't give me more of this, Ezra."

"More of what?"

"It's always a story with you."

"Is that how you feel?"

"You lied to me."

"I know, I'm sorry—"

"Is that it?"

"Narnie. Edem and I don't just share weird ancestral ties. He's my father's half brother. And because of an old town statute, he was given the property when my father went to prison."

I stood there, my mind racing with so many thoughts that I could barely keep up. Maybe I should have listened to Bella; maybe I should've run away from him then. But I played with the tips of his fingers. "What happened that night?"

"My dad won't tell me. He doesn't say much these days. But I know that he was framed, Narnie. I know it. I know that he would never do something like this."

It was precisely then that the bell rang, signalling the end of a period. As the sound of chatter suffused the hallway, I saw Bella approaching us from the corner of my eye. She tilted her head my way, revealing her eyes, bloodshot and swollen and blinking back tears. "Micah's been hospitalized," she breathed out, rushing toward me. "Micah, Narnie. Fucking Micah."

I felt my heart drop to the pit of my stomach as I dropped my hand from Ezra's. "What happened?"

"It was just an hour ago," she trailed off. "Mr. Nelson found him, coughing up blood. It was somewhere in town—I don't know."

"Bella," I murmured, squeezing past Ezra to rush to her side. I draped my arms around her shaking body, glancing at him apologetically. He nodded in understanding.

"He couldn't breathe, Narnie," she sobbed into my shoulder. "You should have seen him lying there, so powerless. And this is Micah we're talking about. Fucking Micah."

Ezra took a step toward her. "Bella—"

"Fuck, I'm so sorry you have to see me like this, Ezra. I'm a mess."

"Don't sweat it, Bella. We're here for you. You know that."

She sighed, attempting to straighten herself. She tried to wriggle free of me, but I didn't let her.

"Micah's going to be okay, Bels," I said.

I let her cry into my shoulder until we were both soaked in her tears. When she calmed down, she asked me if I could go visit him—keep him company. "Mom's stuck in Fort Montgomery with a dead engine and I need to go pick her up. The loser's all alone in the hospital."

"Bella, hey. I can drive to Fort Montgomery," Ezra said. "You go with Narnie."

"In your Harley? Mom would panic."

He scratched the back of his neck.

"What about me?" I offered. "Can I go?"

"Thank you both, but I'll go. I already have a ride. If you can, can you go to the hospital?"

We nodded—and that was how we found ourselves driving through the chilly October evening to a hospital on the other side of town. I found Micah nestled under a blanket, watching Charlie Chaplin on the hospital's barely functioning television screen.

"My love," he said, plastering a cheeky smile on his face. But he faltered. Did he think he could fool me?

I stumbled to his side. I wanted to ask him what had happened, if he was okay—if Edem had done this to him. Instead, a meager "What the hell is this, Micah?" came out.

He looked around the room, his eyes focusing on Ezra. "Where's Bella?"

"She isn't here," I said.

"She didn't come?"

"She's picking up your mom in Fort Montgomery."

He looked down at his hands. "Can you close the door for a second, Ezra?"

I felt my breathing labor as Ezra obliged. "What is it?" I pressed. Was this it—was this the moment he told us he was attacked?

"Ezra Parker," Micah said, shaking his head in amusement. "You sure get around, don't you?"

Ezra lifted his head in acknowledgement, his face indecipherable.

"I was wondering who took that book from Edem's library that night. And what a relief it was to see it peeking out of your backpack this morning."

My body grew hot. He knew about Edem?

A faint smile graced Micah's face. "Siddhartha. It was her favorite, right?"

Ezra's perplexed eyes met Micah's. "You knew Clara?"

"For fuck's sake, Ezra, did you know your sister at all?"

He cast his eyes downward in shame, as if to say no—no he didn't.

"Clara never told you about the band? About The Nuclear Family?"

At Ezra's silence, Micah nodded to himself. "I see." Then he faced me. "And what about you? How come you're spending so much time with this goon?"

I sighed. "What do you know, Micah?"

"You ever wonder why your Mama brought you back here so suddenly, Narnie? I'm quite sure Maya Larson didn't just do it because she missed her husband. She's always been a woman of her own will, hasn't she? And me—did you ever wonder why I came here even when my life was already set, back in San City?"

Because of Clara, I wanted to say, but my mouth churned with a sudden nausea, preventing me from uttering a single word.

"These disappearances—they're all linked, Narnie," he said sadly. "Fighting for her is the last thing I can do before I go."

I swallowed, shakily meeting his eye. "Before you go?"

A melancholy smile graced his face. "Apparently I have some disease. Cancer or something. It's terminal."

I felt my entire world come to a standstill. "Does Bella know?"

He shook his head. "A clueless wonder, isn't she? She'll do anything to stay in that blissful world of hers."

Ezra, who had been silent all this time, released a sigh, the gesture taking us both by surprise. When I turned to face him, I saw that he was on the verge of an emotion I could not deduce. It was sadness—it was longing; it was remorse. "Tell her, Micah," he said tentatively. "Tell her before it's too late, before she spends her entire life resenting you for not giving her those last moments. Tell her unless you want to destroy her."

"Can we have a moment alone, Narnie?" Micah asked me. "Ezra and I."

I nodded, taking my cue to leave the room. It was the longest twenty minutes of my life: the twenty minutes that I spent on the corridor, waiting for the two to finish. When Ezra reopened the hospital door, I was relieved to see that the conversation had taken a turn for the better. The austerity suddenly gone, it seemed that Micah wanted nothing other than to watch Charlie Chaplin.

And for the remainder of the evening, that was exactly what we did.

CHaPTer 7

Today was another day of arriving home long past curfew. Nana was in the living room, sipping tea and watching Elf. I walked into the kitchen without a word. When I walked back to the living room carrying nothing but Kinder ice cream, she looked up from her movie. "Long day?"

I rubbed my eyes, slightly nodding.

"Maya had to go to San City in a work emergency. She left you risotto."

I nodded again, murmuring a vague "Okay" before lumbering up to my bedroom. I did not want Micah to die—not like Papa. I closed my door behind me, my blood pounding in my ears as I relived the memory of that day: a hanging telephone, left abandoned in a scarlet walled living room, the humdrum voice of a government agent on the other end of the line and my mother's stoic countenance as she clutched her hands to her chest. And to think that Bella would get that very same call one day from an absolute stranger to deliver the news that the one person she loved most had passed away. How could I keep this from her? How could I expect her to forgive me?

As I lay down on my bed, I saw Mrs. Henry comforting Mr. Henry through my bedroom window. His body betrayed by grief, he clutched onto his dear wife as if she were at risk of fading away. Above them, the violet sky glistened exquisitely, uncaring of their grief. Only occasionally interrupted by the flashing of the distant radio towers, the sky appeared muddled because of the moisture trapped between my window panes.

I pulled out my phone, googling Does cancer have a cure? I ignored the search results that said no—that certain treatments could work, but there was no agreed upon miracle potion that could get rid of it for good. Maybe this was temporary; maybe his doctors had miscalculated—or maybe this was merely a joke he was playing on all of us.

I found my thoughts interrupted by the sight of Bella walking into her house. With a heavy heart, I slipped out of bed and into my windbreaker. Grabbing my melting tub of ice cream, I slid onto the roof.

The night was crisp with the gentle flare of street lamps illuminating the shedding trees. As I finished my ice cream, I took in the smell of mildew—of the suburban night, gentle and graceful against this callous world. I was mindlessly browsing through my Instagram when a flicker of red sliced through the stillness. In the distance, not too far from the abbey, two silhouettes were setting fire to a nearby statue.

I drew my attention to the arsonists, stopping dead on my tracks when I came across an unsuspecting Sienna Flores. She pulled out a spray paint from her satchel and wrote Justice to Cora Willis along the ashes. As I zoomed in on the figure beside her, I found the blue eyes of Anderson Flemming. I pulled out my phone to record the two. Anderson, realizing the third presence among them, suddenly grabbed Sienna and bolted.

I made an anonymous call to the fire brigade as I watched the fire devour the surrounding cascades of trees. They arrived in seconds, as if they had been waiting endlessly for that call—as if the arsons enshrined them with purpose in this lousy town where nothing exciting ever happened.

I fell asleep to the sound of sirens. And the first thing I did the next morning was pull Anderson into an empty classroom. "You have to explain," I pleaded, letting go of him. "And don't tell me some made up bullshit because I swear, I will see right through it."

His lips trembled, forming an involuntary grimace. "It's complicated."

"Has it been you two all along?"

"Pleading the fifth on that one."

"For fuck's sake, Anderson. Your lives could be ruined if you're found out."

"You think we don't know that? Especially now, with you having that footage. We're fucked."

"You don't have to do this—"

"—but we do, Larson," he said angrily. It was the first time he had taken me by my last name. It took me by surprise. "You haven't been in this shitty town for long enough to know how bad things are around here. These girls—they're disappearing day after day. How many more until something is finally done about it?"

"Anderson," I began.

"Don't. Have you been keeping up with the news at all? The sheriffs haven't investigated a single one of these cases. The fires—they're our form of protest."

"The fires are destroying town property."

"The town can rebuild the goddamn property. But these girls—we can never have them back."

"I don't know what to say."

"Say that you'll delete the video."

"Anderson, I—"

He leaned against the wall, saying nothing.

"If you really are doing this for the girls, why are you so afraid of being seen?"

He hesitated for the longest time before he finally said: "It's complicated."

"Complicated. That word again."

"It takes a lot to be the spokesperson of the cause."

"You think anything comes easy? All those years ago when Malcolm X and Harriet Tubman and all of these revolutionaries put their lives in danger to fight for what is right, you think they wanted it?"

"I don't need a civics lesson from you, Narnie."

"Then what's so complicated, Anderson? What's so complicated about all of this?"

"I can't talk about this anymore," he said softly, releasing a defeated sigh. "Please give me your word that you'll keep this between us."

"But—"

"Please, Narnie."

"Okay."

An understanding passed between the two of us. He left before I could ask him to atone for his past with Bella. As a stream of students flooded the classroom, I brushed past them, my wandering eyes scanning the hallway for his distinctly athletic figure. "Wait, Anderson," I shouted. I waited for the students to slip into their classrooms until it was just the two of us, standing with Sienna Flores by her locker.

"I guess we're royally fucked, aren't we?" she said, laughing to herself.

"You don't have to worry," I said.

"It's hard not to worry when you have footage that can literally destroy our lives."

Anderson released a sigh. "Narnie's fine, Sien. She's good."

"I don't trust her. Not until she deletes that video."

"I will if Anderson tells me what happened between him and Bella," I said before I could think.

Sienna froze, her dark eyes ricocheting between Anderson and I. "Isabella?" she repeated as if her ears had deceived her. "Isabella Henry?"

Anderson's distant eyes found mine.

"Did something happen?" Sienna asked, observing the two of us suspiciously.

"Sienna, nothing happened," he tried to reason.

She narrowed her eyes at me. "I see you just love butting in other people's businesses, Larson." Sighing, she glanced at the clock. "If there isn't anything else, I'm late for class."

"Go, sweetie," Anderson said. "I'll see you there."

"What about you two?"

"We'll be out of here soon."

"And the video?"

"We have her word."

She nodded, slightly relieved. "Alright, see you, Andy."

And then Sienna was gone and Anderson was cornering me, shoving me against the locker. I observed the veins on his neck as his palms collided with the locker behind me. "No more questions," he demanded. "No more questions about Isabella."

With that, he left as well, leaving me with more than just a speculation about his feelings for my best friend.

CHAPTER 8

The day unfolded as many days do: slowly and with a disturbing stillness. Only occasionally interrupted by the ringing of the school bell, I was relieved when it was over. As I grabbed my duffel bag from the girl's locker room and exited onto the field, I was surprised to find Bella waiting for me by the bleachers. "Please tell me Sienna's recent tweets are shitposts and you didn't actually ask Anderson about me today," she said. She released a sigh. "Don't give me that look, Narnie Larson. You know exactly what you did."

"I wanted to see if he still has feelings for you," I said, not knowing what else to say.

"Narnie," she groaned.

"—and he clearly seems to, so what's the problem?"

"What you did wasn't right."

"But he—"

"No, no buts. We hate him. He's old news. End of story."

"But—"

Bella gave me a look.

"Okay, okay. We hate him."

She angrily took my duffel bag into her arms. I felt a pang of guilt at her indignance. Was I really this oblivious; had I hurt Bella so much without even realizing it; I was capable of that—me, Narnie Larson, who in my head wouldn't hurt a fly?

"I'm sorry, Bella," I began, but she released another, equally defeated sigh.

"I understand that you two are friends, but please don't mention me anymore. I don't want to become just another talking point for you two. And especially not for Sienna Flores."

"I won't. I promise."

"I believe you."

Did she really? I worried that she never would—but I had a tendency to exaggerate my wrongdoings, to paint myself as more horrible than I actually was when I hurt those I cared about. I was practicing another apology in my head when Sol Flores approached the two of us. Bella and I exchanged a terse glance as she greeted Bella with a curt nod. She then turned to me. "Hey Narn, any plans tonight?"

Pitted between Sol and Bella and their harrowing history, I bit my lip. "Ye—" I began, but when Bella's scowl deepened, I quickly fixed myself. "Uh, no, no plans?"

Sol wasn't born yesterday. She knew exactly what she was doing, but it didn't seem to phase her. "It's Mateo's birthday and we're throwing a surprise party for him. Nothing big, just a little celebration. You want to come?"

I looked at Bella again, seeing past her stoic countenance the dismay forming in her eyes. I knew then that going to the party tonight would be a horrible idea. I would rather be in the hospital anyway, watching reruns of poorly directed romantic comedies with Bella and Micah.

"Ezra will be there," Sol added.

"I mean if Ezra will be there," Bella chimed in. "I guess she has to go."

"Come on, Bel. Don't mock me like that."

"We're late to see Micah," Bella said, releasing a sigh.

Sol grabbed her wrist, stopping her. "See Micah?" she asked curiously. When Bella brushed herself off without an explanation, Sol faced me. "Did something happen?"

"He's—" I began while Bella said "None of your business" at the same time. I stopped myself.

"He's what?" Sol repeated with concern.

Bella rolled her eyes. "Like you care. Narnie, are we going?"

"Come tonight, Narnie," Sol said softly. "Mateo would really appreciate it."

"I'll think about it," I said. "I'll text you."

We exchanged a brief goodbye before I caught up with Bella. "Easy there, Bel."

"Go to the party," she said. "Like, don't not go on my account. I need some alone time with Micah without your distracting ass anyway."

"Are you sure?"

"If you ask me again, I won't be."

So I found myself sliding into Sol's old pickup truck later that night. We drove silently until we saw a sign to the interstate. She stole a glance at me from the periphery of her eye. "Hey, who would've thought, right?" she finally said.

I unrolled the window, resting my elbow on the ledge. "Thought what?"

"That we'd be in my car like this, actually hanging out—I don't know. I'm just trying to make conversation."

I closed the window as we entered the highway and the noise became too much to bear. "I'm sorry for whatever happened between you and Bella."

She stared directly ahead. "She can't fathom me."

"Does it have anything to do with Micah?"

She laughed at me—at my naivety, I suppose. "Bella hasn't told you?" She merged onto the slower lane despite the desolate roads. "It's a long story."

"Do you want to talk about it?"

"Someone's curious."

"Maybe, just a little."

"There isn't really much to say. We were all just old friends, way back when."

"I see."

"It was years ago. Before Micah left. I hear he's back now?"

"He has been, for a while now."

"Yeah. I've been watching Bel's Instagram stories."

"Were you two close?"

"Something like that."

"Bella mentioned it in passing."

"God, she must hate me."

"I wouldn't say that, Sol."

"And Micah..."

She was unable to hide the smile on her lips as she spoke about Micah.

They met when she was eleven. She was in fifth grade at the time and Bella's closest friend. When Bel graduated as the valedictorian of their class and her parents threw a party for their prodigy, Sol found herself standing before him on their veranda. Micah had come to the door to greet her—her, with her thick, wired braces and hair meshed into tight pigtails. "Hello there," she said, meeting his anticipating gaze. She tugged at her hair.

Micah softened, the corners of his lips trembling into a smile.

A faint blush creeping onto her cheeks, she motioned toward her hands. "I bought these," she said, extending her arms to show him the gift. "It's a scrapbook collection for Isabella."

Micah opened the door wide enough for her to enter. "So give it to her."

"That's what I was gonna do," she replied indignantly.

He held the door for her as she walked in. "Bella's in the kitchen."

"After that, it became frequent, my visits to Bella's, and Micah would be there, him and his friends. You know how it is. You become Bel's friend and Micah basically comes with the package.

"It wasn't long before we were spending long, quality time together. It was exhilarating, being around him. With Teo and Bella, it was calm. We were too young to do anything with our lives. But Micah—nothing seemed to satisfy him. He was always going around, looking for his next big adventure.

Sol clutched her books to her chest as she walked alongside Isabella. February. Four years ago. They were bracing to cross the road when his jeep sliced their vision, with his friends tucked inside like prophets. She saw him standing with his head poking out of the passenger's seat. His hands were touching the sky.

"Going somewhere, baby sister?" he shouted at Isabella.

Bella raised her head to acknowledge him, curling her lips into a scowl. "Sod off!"

He smiled mischievously at Sol before the jeep sped away. Her body gathered warmth, goosebumps rising in the wake of her arms.

Bella narrowed her eyes at her best friend. "Should I ask?"

That was grade eight.

Grade nine was when Sol began rehearsing what she would say to him in her bedroom vanity. She wondered what she could say to captivate him on the Tuesdays their paths collided on her way to first period, when she would see him gently strumming his guitar in the choir hall that fell on her way.

He would glance at the door as she passed him. It was like he could sense her presence somehow, like he knew she was there without the slightest indication.

She would wave at him and he would smile at her and that was their thing.

She remembered the little things about him, like how Micah loved to play folk music whenever the weather was kind—and how could she forget his penchant for strumming along to Marble Floors on rainy mornings? One day when the door was slightly open, she walked in on him playing The Beatles. Last night's downpour had subsided by the morning. Micah was playing Here Comes the Sun.

"It's my favorite by them," she said, closing the door behind her. Her heart fluttered like a madwoman at the realization that they were alone.

He smiled in appreciation between his singing. When he finished, she staged a standing ovation for him. "Your voice, Micah. It's not made for this town."

"Where's it made for then, love?"

"For somewhere better."

So it became a routine for Sol to be late to her freshman seminar. She much preferred to stay with him anyway. He would play for her, one song after another. She listened eagerly, providing him with enthusiasm every time. One of those days he invited her to Fort Montgomery to watch him play.

When the long anticipated night finally arrived, she was ashamed that the traffic had caused her to be late. When the local bus stopped her by the venue, she saw people streaming out of it until it was at last empty. She whisked in without thinking, breathless and in disarray, and scanned the café for him. He was dismantling his microphone on the stage, his eyes lost in concentration. She walked briskly and with a resolve, and when she was just beneath him, he glanced downward, noticing her.

A coy smirk toyed on his lips at the sight of her restlessness. "Where's the fire, Solita?"

"There was traffic."

"It's alright," he said, picking apart the cable. "I admire the effort."

Fighting the hollowness growing in her chest, she conjured every fiber of being to pull herself onto the stage. "Did it go well?" she asked, a meager attempt at conversation.

He nodded curtly. "Yeah."

"Yeah?"

"Yes, Solita," he repeated—and he looked at her for the first time that night, his dimpled smile assuring her that maybe things were okay after all.

She folded a microphone stand and gave it to him, their fingers caressing in translation. They worked in silence until Micah's bandmates emerged from the back of the stage. They were a group of three: Roman, Anderson and—

"Anderson?" I asked, interrupting her. "Anderson Flemming?"

"Yeah. Anderson was in the band. He was different back then though, like really different."

"Different how?"

"We were kids, Narnie. Things changed over the years. We had to consider things we once didn't have to."

"We?"

"He. I meant he. His father became really sick a few years ago. Trapped the kid by saying it was his dream to see his son follow in his footsteps and become a professional footballer. They didn't approve of the music."

"That's horrible..."

"Yeah, I mean, don't get me wrong. He's doing great. He's excelling in football. He's already got an offer from San City University, to go on an athletic scholarship. But he's not happy."

"How could he be? He's so stupid, throwing his dreams away, just like that."

"Micah was the complete opposite. He had a dream and he abandoned us for it."

"Sol..."

"I'm fine. Don't worry. I've had a long time to get over him."

"Was it just the three of them? Micah, Anderson and Roman?"

"And Clara."

"Clara?"

"Yeah, Clara. Why?"

I thought about Ezra's sister Clara, the Clara Micah had returned for. "No reason."

"They were some of the most incredible people I've ever met. I think it's one of the best things Micah did for me, introducing me to them.

They spent the night together, the four of them, until it was time to call it a night. As everyone returned to their prospective rides, she found herself clustered with Micah in the parking lot of the venue. It was just the two of them—and his burning cigarette. When he offered it to her, she took it with ease. Micah would never know that Sol had never smoked before. He would never know that her first time had been with him. The first of many firsts and of many lasts.

They talked freely, conquering the silence that accompanied many new beginnings with ease. After finishing the cigarette, they returned to the venue: a dainty coffeehouse that suited the two. A gentle acoustic emerged from the vintage jukebox as they settled for a conversation over a cup of bitter coffee—no cream or sweeteners, the only way he took it, she would later come to know. She hated bitter coffee, but the possibility of a future with him made it more bearable.

They talked about their past and their future, about their remorse and what they wanted out of life. "I feel like I'm transgressing just a little, like I shouldn't enjoy being with my baby sister's best friend this much," he said sometime that night.

She rested her chin on her palm, smiling at him. "I feel like I shouldn't enjoy being with my best friend's older brother this much either."

"And yet, here we are."

Indeed, there they were, indulging in each other with a childlike interest, neither aware of the sanctuary they would find in each other in the years to come.

Sol took a sip of her coffee, tucking a strand of her hair behind her ear. Micah loved it when she did that. It prompted the clearest view of her porcelain face. It reminded him of a cloudless sunset, every color sharp against the canvas that was her skin. He looked at her, biting his lower lip to resist a smile as he counted the freckles dotting her scarlet cheeks like stars. Her eyes may have been the sea, a stark and astounding blue. Micah found himself submerged in their depth.

"This is my favorite song," she said as a Frankie Vallie song began to play.

He listened. And then he began to sing.

"Micah," she began with a laugh.

"Can't take my eyes off of you," he continued. He left his coffee on the table and pulled her into a dance. And the coffee must have grown cold, but their bodies brimmed with warmth as he twirled her around, their laughter filling the empty coffeeshop. When the song drew an end, she ran to their table and pulled a polaroid out of her purse. Running back to the jukebox where Micah was, she took a photo of the two of them, their bodies light with delight and their red cheeks pressed against the other's.

"We left that place a little after ten," Sol said. "We were the last ones out."

The car ride was fleeting. They had carpooled with a group of townies. Because Micah hadn't accounted for Sol, the only seat she could afford was on his lap. She sat there in silence, her body rigid against his as they drove across Fort Montgomery.

They got off on the corner of Frazier and Nelson. Micah walked her home. Once on her doorstep, her eyes met his. "Thank you for tonight," she said, stepping onto her doormat.

"Thank you for coming."

"Thank you for inviting me."

"Thank you for staying after."

"Thank you for letting me."

"Goodnight Solita."

With that, he let her go. He was really good at that, at taking her to her doorstep and so quickly letting her go. It made her wonder if he felt anything for her at all.

It was nearly two years later, as she was approaching the end of her sophomore year and Micah finishing his freshman year at a local university, that she confronted him about it. It had been after one of his gigs. They were by the water with his bandmates:

Roman, Anderson and Clara. That day, Bella had tagged along, tethering herself to Anderson's side. They had grown to be quite close.

The wooden boardwalk prompted a glorious view of the city across the sea. Skyscrapers lined Fort Montgomery in the distant horizon. In the velvety ground across the water, cars drifted with the guidance of faint streetlights, weaving in and out of the fabric of chilly air. Every building was a silhouette from afar, marked in enigma.

Sol spotted Micah sitting on the edge, his feet dangling close to the water. Her body challenged her to approach him, to say something to him, but she remained on the pavement, eying him from afar. She took in the soft bronze of his skin and his large hands, wondering how it would feel to be touched by them.

He noticed the lingering presence eventually. He looked behind his shoulder, raising an eyebrow. She walked to the edge of the boardwalk, occupying the space next to him.

"Anderson was playing this song by Dawn Golden," she recalled wistfully. "That was around the time his dad got sick—and the townies would torment him. Like, how are you ever going to make it as a footballer or a musician with two hundred pounds on you? He had left the band already, but it was that summer that he left music altogether."

"And I know I'm hard to take,

And my bones are calling out your name.

Because you're all that I, all that I want."

"I feel like The Nuclear Family is going to hit it big one day," Sol murmured to Micah, observing Anderson in the distance. He was sitting on a wooden log with Bella beside him. Her chin was perched on her palms, her eyes glowing at his concentrated face as he plucked the strings of his guitar. "Just look at him, Micah."

Micah looked behind his shoulder at Anderson, saying nothing.

"You think you can convince him to join you guys again?"

"The Nuclear Family's dead, Sol."

"Listen, I know Anderson. I know that if you just try a little harder to convince him—"

"It's not about Anderson this time," he added quickly, as if that would make the pain any less.

She faltered. "What do you mean?"

"I'm leaving Holden."

Her eyes widened.

"I was accepted into that really competitive accelerated law program. The one in San City. I can't stay here anymore, not unless I want to rot here too."

She looked at him—really looked at him, at his beautiful face that she was already beginning to miss. An indecipherable expression had crossed his face. "Did you already accept the transfer?"

"Yeah."

They lapsed into a momentary silence, Anderson's voice soft against the gentle lapping of waves. "I don't know what to say."

"I paid my deposit today."

"What's wrong with the program in Port Orion though, Micah?"

"There's a universe out of here, Flores," he said, looking away. "Out of this fucking town, there's too much to discover."

I don't want you to go, she wanted to say. She wanted to pull him into a hug, but instead she pulled herself together, fighting the lump forming in her throat. "I'm happy for you."

His mouth seemed to have caught on glue, as he said nothing.

"Some nerve of him, after all those years," she muttered, her voice slightly cracking. "We all knew Micah was going to leave us, but we didn't think he would do it so soon. He had his undergrad—he had three more years. And what hurt the most was his indifference. He was leaving for good and all I could think about was the beautiful women he was going to meet in San City but it didn't seem to matter to him that he was leaving me. And I was going to tell him.

She really was going to tell him. If only she could find the right words.

Micah placed his hand on her thigh. "I'll miss you, Solita."

They were always like this, straddling a dangerous boundary between becoming something and staying as the platonic friends they were. Was this all they were condemned to be?

"Prove it," she said angrily, and the next succession of events unraveled in a blur. One minute they were apart and then they weren't anymore, meshing in a synchronicity that Sol had not even in her wildest daydreams dared to imagine. His lips danced on hers with the ardent passion they had been suppressing their entire lives. And for a second, she was sure he would never let go.

But he did, leaving behind nothing more than the subtle traces of his evening coffee on her lips. He gave her a weak "I can't," and she felt Isabella's eyes on them from afar, her lips drawn apart in shock at the sight of her brother and her best friend.

Tears clouded her vision as she stood up from there. Carrying the humiliation that she had feared the most for the last six years, she bolted. Shoving past the foliage and currents of racing cars, she let her feet carry her until she was far away—far from Micah and Bella and everyone she knew.

She looked straight ahead, her lips pressed in a thin line of indignation. "He broke my heart. And now he's back. And all I've wanted to do is see him again. Talk about how much we've both grown. Ask if he'd ever want to give things another shot—"

"Jesus, Sol," I said, the realization dawning on me that it was Micah she had wanted to text all those nights ago, in her truck.

"It's so ridiculous. I know. But I know he's not okay. Bella had that look, the I'm-slowly-losing-my-mind look she gets when something's wrong. I don't know. Maybe it's all in my head. And I can't just ask her, because when things ended with Micah, I ended things with her too. Because she's a living copy of him and god, it hurts to look at someone you love and to see in them someone who destroyed you."

"I'm so sorry, Sol."

"It's not your fault, darling."

"Do you miss her?"

She pulled her car into Teo's driveway, checking her watch. "Of course I do. But I'm afraid I've shared a little too much tonight. And I haven't even had a drink yet. Shall we go in?"

I nodded, taking her lead. Once at the door, I squeezed her arm. "It's going to be okay, Sol. I don't know how, but it is. I promise."

She smiled weakly, reaching for the doorbell.

Everyone else was already there: Teo's family and his closest friends, Anderson and Sienna. Surrounded by their company, I felt like I had a family again. I felt like Papa was still here, like he was alive in the benign actions of the people around me: in Teo's mother, Margarita, who was fixing a fallen banner and in his father, Teodor, who was tending to the roasted potatoes in the oven.

At eight o' seven, the doorbell finally rang, signalling Teo's arrival. Teo's mom lit the candles as Sol opened the door.

"Happy birthday!" we shouted. We faltered when we saw Ezra.

"Sorry I'm late," he said sheepishly.

Sol pulled him in, closing the door behind him. "Ugh, Ezra, hurry. Teo's supposed to be here any minute now. Okay, Margarita, lights off again please!"

Teo's mother, Margarita, nodded, turning off the lights. Just then, the doorbell rang again. The lights flickered back on for a fleeting moment before Sol peered through the peephole and whispered, "It's him!"

Margarita dimmed the lights again. As Sol opened the door, everybody began to sing. I joined in as well, observing Teo as he walked inside, his cheeks pink from the cold and his hair slightly disheveled. "Happy birthday, dear Teo. Happy birthday to you."

Sol slipped to his side, kissing his cheek. "Make a wish, handsome man."

He laughed, closing his eyes and blowing the candles.

"What did you wish for?" she asked him later that night.

He brought his fingers to her chin, rubbing it softly. "You really want to know?"

She nodded eagerly.

"I wished for these moments to never end."

She found me shortly after, engrossed in conversation with Mateo's cousin, Felipe. "A bunch of us are going to the lake with our skates," she said. "The water's apparently frozen solid. You want to come?"

"Hell yeah," I said.

It snowed as we loaded ourselves into her truck. Anderson, Ezra and I fixed ourselves on the backseat while Teo rode in the front with her. He adjusted his phone to the auxiliary cord. As an Arcade Fire song began to play, I saw Anderson scroll through Bella's Instagram story. She was in town with a brown haired townie from calculus.

Anderson pushed her off his screen. "Mateo, you talk to Nate lately?"

I saw Sol's eyebrows furrow in the rearview mirror.

"No," Teo answered. "Why?"

"Saw he was in town."

I gently tugged on Ezra's jacket. He was leaning against the window, sleepily watching the snowflakes disappear into the dimly lit suburban night. His eyes fluttered toward me.

"You okay?" I asked him.

"Yeah. Why wouldn't I be?"

"You're quiet."

"It's 'cause you were flirting with Felipe earlier, Narnie," Sol said with a smirk. "Your boyfriend feels neglected."

"Shut up, Sol," I said while Teo said, "Felipe? Seriously? My cousin Felipe?"

All the warmth in my body surged to my face.

"Cut her some slack, Teo," Sol said. "We've all been there."

"By we you mean you?"

"He's half French," she deadpanned, as if that explained everything.

"My dad was French," Ezra said.

Sol arched an eyebrow. "Really?"

"Yeah, but Mom's not. She's from Beirut."

"Explains the killer genes," I said teasingly.

Sol giggled. "Oh my, things are getting steamy back there, aren't they?"

Ezra placed his hand on my thigh. "What about you?"

"I'm a halfie too. Mom's Nepali and my dad's a plain old Holden man."

"Holden?" Sol repeated. "Seriously? I can't believe your beautiful Nepali mother married some dude from Holden. She could have married a Frenchman."

Teo leaned into Sol's dashboard, lowering the music. "Do you still have family in Nepal, Narnie?"

"My mom's entire family is back there, actually."

"Really?"

"Uh huh. Do you know Annapurna?"

"The mountain range?"

"Yeah, they live in a village not too far from there."

"Are you close to them?"

"Not particularly. Most of them don't speak English. And—"

"—you don't speak Nepali," Ezra finished, squeezing my thigh.

"You too?"

He nodded. "Mom and Dad moved here when they were still young. She had a very turbulent relationship with her family. So I never got to meet them. And maybe it is meaningless to think about her life back then. But I still can't shake the feeling that a meaningful part of my identity was taken away from me because of her decision, you know?"

"I understand, Ezra," I said. I understood it so much. I wish I had been closer to Mama's family too.

"Oh my god, let's plan a trip!" Sol said all of a sudden. "Let's go to Nepal and then Lebanon. When we graduate, in June, let's find your families, you poor souls."

"A pre-college adventure," Teo said reflectively. "Fuck, I'm so down."

Ezra chuckled. "I can pick up extra shifts at work."

Sol's eyes flickered toward Anderson. "Anderson?"

Anderson was still on his phone, scrolling through Instagram.

"Andy?" she repeated softly.

"Um, travel to Lebanon in June?" he said. "Yeah. Sure."

Ezra and I exchanged glances. When we reached the lake, he pulled his hand away from my thigh, leaving goosebumps where there was once warmth. We pulled the skates out of Sol's hood and ran to the lake, Anderson the only one of us who stayed behind.

The ice glimmered under the callow glow of the moon. It is precisely a decade later that I am standing before that very lake, yearning for that chilly night when I wondered if I was falling in love for the very first time. The snow cloaked the meadow around us with a silver sheen. I breathed nimbly into the air, the smell of the nearby pines calming my senses as I struggled to balance on the ice.

Around me, the sound of Sol's carefree laughter filled the vicinity. She was circling the lake with Teo, both of them on their skates. Anderson was sitting on the hood of her truck, gazing into the open sky. Ezra snuck beside me, taking my hand into his. "You don't know how to skate, do you?"

I flushed in embarrassment. No, I didn't...

"Give me your hand."

My fingers relapsed into his like a traveler finding her way home after a long journey. As I sought refuge in his gaze, I felt for the first time in my life that I had a reason to believe in god. He pulled me into him before pushing me away again.

"Ezra," I groaned, my breath clouding the air before me. "What are you doing?"

He chuckled, helping me to regain my balance. "What's your favorite song?"

"I have so many."

"The first one that comes to your head?"

"I don't know. I guess—um, Love is a laserquest? By Arctic Monkeys."

"Close your eyes."

I obliged despite my fear that he would let go.

"Sing it for me."

"I'm a horrible singer."

"Please?"

I hesitated—but when I opened my eyes again, he was staring at me with his soft, anticipating gaze. How could I refuse? I closed my eyes as I began to sing. "Do you still feel younger than you thought you would by now? Or darling, have you started feeling old yet? Don't worry, I'm sure that you're still breaking hearts, with the efficiency that only youth can harness..."

A small smile gracing his face, he let go of one of my hands and twirled me around with the other. "And do you still think love is a Laserquest?" he joined in. "Or do you take it all more seriously?"

"I've tried to ask you this in some daydreams that I've had," we continued. "But you're always busy being make-believe..."

"Open your eyes," Ezra said.

I opened my eyes to find myself gliding along the ice, the wind dancing on my cheeks. Ezra was just inches away, his face glistening with pride. "You did it, Narnie."

My knees trembled at his words. He was still looking at me with those eyes. Swallowed by his gaze, I suddenly felt the weight of gravity anchoring me to the ground—or maybe I was wrong. Maybe it was fate anchoring me to him. I fell onto the ice with Ezra beneath me, my warm breath pooling onto his nose. We were trapped in time again, Ezra and I. The sound of Sol's laughter vanished into thin air.

I wanted to tell him everything then. I wanted to tell him how I felt when I saw him on the bleachers in late August, reading Man's Search for Meaning, and how I had not forgotten him since. And how these past few months had gone by in chaos, but when it was all over, maybe we could finally go on a date. A real one. Maybe in town, in Stella's diner, discussing books over canadian omelettes and a warm cup of cappuccino.

He brought his fingers to my face, brushing away a solitary strand of hair. "Has anyone ever told you how beautiful you are?"

"Only Mama."

He chuckled again, burying his hands at the nape of my neck. I thought about his pretty eyed lady, the victim of his frequent nostalgia, and wondered if I could make him forget her. Did he remember her then? I felt my insides churn at the thought that I could never compare.

"Hey Ezra?"

"Yeah?"

"What do you think of me?"

"What I think of you," he contemplated, laughing into my face. I felt his soft lips brush against my nose. "I enjoy you so much."

"Hey you two!" Sol shouted, snapping us out of our reverie. "Apparently the blizzard's picking up. Margarita and Teodor want us back."

I pulled away from him wondering what we were.

"Am I dropping you two home?" Sol asked as we returned to her car.

Ezra scratched the back of his neck. "My ride is still at Teo's."

"Maybe you guys can stay the night tonight?" Teo suggested. "It doesn't feel right to let you head back in this storm."

"I'll text Nana," I said, pulling out my phone. As I texted her, I slipped into the backseat of Sol's car, following Anderson and Ezra.

"Unfortunately I can't stay," Ezra said. "I have work in the morning."

Teo looked behind his shoulder at him. "Even if there's Fireball?"

"Even if there's Fireball."

Sol rolled her eyes. "Fake news, Ezra."

"Come on, Sol. You know I want to stay."

"Whatever. Pray that the car doesn't slip on ice," she said, buckling her seatbelt.

The drive back to Teo's place stretched on indefinitely because of the icy roads. I lay my head on Ezra's shoulder as the minutes drew on. I must have fallen asleep there while around us, the night faded into a lighter dawn. I woke up the next morning in a caravan amid the woods. The world smelled like lavender.

From the corner of my eye, I saw Ezra slide into the bedroom with nothing but a pair of gray sweats on. "Morning sleepyhead."

I rubbed my eyes, groggily sitting up on the bed. "Is this a dream?"

"Does it feel like a dream?"

"Just a little."

"Not a dream, Narnie."

I looked around the narrow vicinity, struggling to make out where we were.

Every corner was meticulously organized, every cabinet a luminous shade of mahogany. The bedroom shared a space with the rest of the caravan. An ornate carpet began where the bedroom met the kitchen, ending just below the bed. I saw Kundera's novels scattered on the dining table beside a bowl of fruit. With a small vase seated amidst its rich wooden frame, the books were all partially open: Ignorance, The Festival of Insignificance, The Unbearable Lightness of Being, The Book of Laughter and Forgetting and Immortality.

Dilapidated bookcases perimetered the sides of the bedroom. Their once rich mahogany shade had darkened throughout the years, each bookcase overflowing with classics and contemporaries, the bridge between then and now.

"Welcome, Narnie, to my humble abode," Ezra said, his cheeks reddening slightly. He looked so delicious in that moment, surrounded by those beautiful books.

"How did we end up here?"

"You don't remember?"

"No."

"We were on our way to Teo's, remember? You fell asleep on the way and you wouldn't wake up. We were going to take you into his guest room, but you latched onto me and kept mumbling something, so Sol drove the two of us here."

I tried to hide my diffidence as I met his eye. "I did that?"

"With your dear life."

"That's so embarrassing."

"I didn't mind."

I looked down at my clothes, blushing as I realized that I was beginning to smell.

"I put clean clothes for you on top of the hamper in the bathroom. They're Clara's. I hope they fit."

I nodded in silent gratitude.

He led me to the bathroom. A silent and fleeting journey. I observed his taut arms on the whole way there, up until the very moment he opened the bathroom door wide enough for me to enter. I came out shortly after smelling like his lavender shampoo, clad in Clara's dark jeans and red turtleneck. I entered the kitchen to find the rich aroma of bergamot and cinnamon filling the air. He was standing by the stove, brewing us tea.

"It smells like Mama's chai," I said, walking up to him.

"Good, because I actually looked up an authentic Nepali recipe."

I felt my heart flutter. "You didn't have to do that."

"I also made omelettes. They're on the table. Do you like omelettes?"

"I love them."

I tried to tame my despotic heart as Ezra strained the tea into cups. On the table lay french toast, omelettes and sliced oranges—and moments later, our chai. He took the seat across from me and sipped his tea. I watched his lips meet the corner of the ceramic cup. When he caught me looking, he arched his eyebrows. I looked away.

He talked about his favorite author, Joe Amendola, and his piece for The Outline about the Great Pacific Garbage Patch being the only wonder our world ever created. He talked about the tragedy of the lives devoured by war and poverty. "It's like Frazier said in Cold Mountain, when Inman returns home after four years out in the battlefield. A long time gone. And it is pointless to think how those years could have been put to better use. But you still can't help but wonder."

"The best we can do now is put our lives to better use, right? Actually fight for the things we believe in."

"We're just kids."

"Maybe that's our biggest mistake. Believing we are just kids."

A small smile invaded his beautiful face. "When did you become such a philosopher?"

"I don't know. But it's nice, you know? Being here with you like this without the world weighing on our shoulders. I feel happy."

"Speaking of which—"

"Micah."

"I can't believe he knows."

"I can't believe he's dying."

He placed his hands on the table, a tightlipped frown settling on his face. "I went to see him yesterday."

"And?"

"He's okay. But Bella isn't doing too good."

"Do you blame her?"

He looked away, saying nothing.

I found that those hours with him passed a little too quickly. Our yearning for a great escape eventually led us to the woods. I borrowed a pair of gloves and a scarf that he had lying around, and we sauntered along the trees that awned over us, leading us to the village. A chilly breeze occasionally shook the forest, causing the branches to shiver under the low, incandescence of the sky. Particles of ice wafted around us like dust vapors, pirouetting along the meadow like little wisps of life fading in and out of focus.

"When I was little, I always wondered why the pines kept their leaves year round," I told Ezra as we walked through the snow. "Papa would tell me it's because they are so sure of what they are that they choose not to shed off and stay as they are until they die."

"Do you see yourself in those trees?"

"I don't know. It's nice to shed every once in a while, no? Pretend you aren't yourself and start all over again."

"In theory."

"Only in theory?"

"You can never really shed off the people that leave their marks on you, can you?"

We wandered around until we saw the first glimpses of suburbia, its cascading houses and faraway valleys—and when it became too cold for us to bear, we found a café to warm ourselves in.

"The caravan was my mother's," he told me as we settled inside Cornelia's. A gentle melody emerged from the jukebox as he motioned us toward a seat by the window. We removed our coats, the aroma of coffee beans fresh in the air. "She bought it because she wanted a mobile home for her travels. But then I was born and she traveled less and less. And we still had this beautiful caravan in our driveway. After turning eighteen in July, it was the only thing I took when I left Edem's."

"How was it, living with Edem?"

"He treated me very well—almost too well, I guess, like he was trying to remedy his guilt through me."

Guilt for what? I wanted to ask. Could redemption truly exist for a crime as severe as murder? But I said nothing.

He reached toward the center of the table for the menu. I observed his brisk movements, the swiftness of his eyes as they explored the glossy paper before him. My hand traveled to his unoccupied ones, taking him by surprise. Why did I do that?

And then he was waiting for me to say something—any-thing—but I sat there, trapped in my own suspense, waiting for my next words. I felt my lips tremble.

"You lovebirds ready to order?" a voice said from beside us. I moved my hand away.

Ezra cast his eyes back to the menu. "A warm nutella please."

He looked at me, at my silence and at my lips that floundered for words.

"Make that two," he amended, handing over the menu.

She took it from him, only to place it back at the center of the table. "Shirley, two warm nutellas for table four please!" she shouted across the café before moving toward the next table. Ezra toyed with the menu, pretending to look it over.

I wanted nothing more than to demolish his sudden restraints. Maybe he had crafted it for his protection after his pretty eyed lady ruined his faith in love. I wanted something more for him, a happier ending away from the melancholy; I wanted to show him the love he deserved—and not just this platonic love he forced upon us in between his flirtatious gestures. I wanted to unravel him completely; I wanted him to let me.

We drank our warm nutellas in silence, pausing every now and again for occasional banter. He walked me home before his afternoon shift. I stared at my ceiling for hours, until my mind became numb with thoughts of the two of us—and until knocks arose from the other side of my door. "Narns?" Nana said softly.

I looked at the door.

"How was Mateo's party?" she asked me, slipping in through the barely open door. She sat at the edge of my bed, releasing a sigh. "You've been running around so much these days. How are you, dear?"

I thought about everything that had happened and entertained the idea of telling her. But I couldn't. "I'm fine, Nana," I finally said.

"Have you thought about where you want to go for college?"

"San City University," I said quickly. "I've already submitted my applications."

"Well," she began, placing her hands on her lap. "Let me know when you hear back. We can have a little celebration, just you, me and Maya. And maybe you can invite your new friends. I'd love to meet them."

"I would love that too, Nana."

She looked straight ahead as silence cradled the room around us. "There's a holiday supper in the abbey tonight," she said eventually. "Will you join me?"

"In the abbey?" I repeated, holding my breath.

"The entire town is supposed to be there. I know we still have a few weeks to go until the holidays, but I think it will be a lot of fun to start the celebrations early."

"Of course I will, Nana," I said. I wondered if she heard the crack in my voice, subtle but inextricable. If she did, she carried on without questioning it. And I let her, rolling over on my bed, wondering what awaited us when we returned to that place: a holy place, a benevolent place, a place that for me had grown to symbolize nothing but terror.

CHAPTER 9

The ride to the abbey was haunting. It was as if darkness had invaded all of Holden, obfuscating the air with uncertainty. As we approached its familiar ivory gates, I told myself that every-thing would be okay—that maybe we were just paranoid, Ezra and I—and that everything was just in our heads. But I couldn't shake the feeling that it wasn't, that something darker awaited us ahead.

I spotted Sol first, standing beside Edem in the congregation hall, immersed in conversation. She was smiling at something he was saying. I wondered if he knew then, that the book was missing. But of course he knew. How could he not know? There was a gap in the bookcase where there had once been Clara Parker's Siddhartha, delineated in his own handwriting.

There was a sermon before the supper. Edem led us through the prayers, his eyes wandering the hall between his recitals. It was like they were searching for something—someone—and when they finally found mine, he paused tentatively, the gesture so cumbersome that it devoured the air in the room with its gravity.

I looked away, struggling for Micah's glance. He was already looking at me, an indecipherable expression plastered on his face. He rolled his eyes, mimicking a gun with his hands and pretending to shoot himself. My heartbeat accelerated as my eyes traveled back to Edem's. He lowered his gaze to the holy book on the podium, an abiding smirk overtaking his face. "Be wary," he began. "In this state of nature, your adversary walks about like an unforgiving wolf, seeking whom he may devour. And the wolf too disguises himself as the lone bearer of good when his motives are far more sinister."

Edem had certainly packaged his identity in that way, fooling even those who knew him best. When the ceremony dawned an end, he directed us to the great hall, where the holiday feast was expected to be. A generous dinner was planted on three long tables lain with glittering plates and golden goblets. As Nana left to socialize with her friends, I found myself across him once again. Slowly, he enclosed the proximity between us. And just when I was sure that I would go mad, he brushed past me, disappearing into the room.

I pressed my palms to my chest as I scavenged the room for him, reminding myself that he was gone. Instead, I ran into Sol. She looked just as unsettled as I did. "Narnie," she said nervously. "I've been looking for you."

I played with the hem of my sleeve.

"Well, it's just—it's my first time seeing him in a long time, you know?" she continued. When I merely gawked at her, wondering if she was talking about Edem, she motioned toward one of the long tables where Micah lay. "He doesn't look so good these days. Why does he look like that, Narnie?"

I sighed. How could I tell her—how could I not tell her?

"Please, Narnie."

"Sol, I—"

"Please."

"He's been sick."

She faltered. "Sick?"

"Talk to him."

Her hands fell limply to her sides. "He doesn't want to talk to me."

"There's nothing else to do, Sol."

"I know. It's just—it's scary. The thought of talking to him again. The thought of closure."

"I wish I could do more, darling."

"No, it's fine. I get it."

"I'm really sorry."

"It's kind of ironic, isn't it?"

"What is?"

"That I have everything, but you are still where I want to be. And it's all because of him."

"Sol..."

She averted her gaze from mine, beginning to leave.

"He still talks about you," I said before she could go.

She froze, her shallow breathing suddenly perceptible despite the cacophony in the room. I wondered what stopped her. Was it hope?

"I could never put the pieces together with you two. But for what it's worth, he's just as miserable as you are."

And was that a smile I suddenly saw grace Sol Flores' lips? She walked away, saying nothing more. I followed her with my eyes. She was back to normal again: to the cheerful Sol who was so unlike the Sol I had come to know in the past few days. I saw her again the next day. "I'm going to do it, Narnie," she declared with a resolve she had never had before. "I'm going to talk to him. And I'm going to fix things with Bella."

We were all in town, decorating the streets in anticipation for the holiday season.

"I'm so happy for you," I said—and I meant it. Because God, all of this was so overdue.

"After I got home last night, I got to thinking," she continued. "And it's all in my hands, isn't it? I mean, the past isn't. Not anymore. But the future—maybe that is."

"Exactly, Sol. Exactly."

Beside us, a group of townies were unloading large cardboard boxes of fairy lights from a truck. Among the group of four, I saw Teo and Anderson. We walked toward them, finding Bella not too far along, angrily speaking to another one of the townies.

The sunlight brightened the streets of the callow morning, but as Sol and I entered the vicinity and Bella's unsuspecting eyes found mine, I saw darkness. I was swept into the indignation that flowed between the two, and in Bella's eyes, I saw war. I saw hope. I saw everything that had been lost and everything that could be saved.

"I'll talk to you later?" Sol said, her eyes wandering away from Bella's.

"Later," I said.

Bella flashed me a brief smile as I caught up to her. "How was the party?"

"It was good," I said. "Can't believe I had to find out from Anderson that you were in town with a fucking townie."

"Wait, what?"

"He was sulking all evening. Nearly ruined our night."

"Shut up, Narnie."

"I'm serious!"

She rolled her eyes.

"Sol told me about that night on the boardwalk. She misses you."

Bella reached for one of the cardboard boxes the townies had left behind.

"What happened between you two?"

"I don't want to rehash it right now."

"Whenever you're ready."

She sighed, kicking the box.

"Bella, I'm here for you. Always. You know that, right?"

"It's just—she really hurt me, Narnie. And it's hard to see her so often. I had sworn her off forever. And Anderson. He chose her."

"What do you mean he chose her?"

Isabella stared directly ahead at the madness unwinding before her: at her best friend's shaky arms removing themselves from the nape of her brother's neck, her eyes flaring with an emotion akin to acrimony as she stood up in haste and then bolting away. Nothing can capture what Bella was feeling then, but sheer astonishment comes close.

She stood up to follow after her friend, but Sol stopped her. "Don't you dare, Bella," she sputtered through her tear stained face, taking her by surprise.

So she chose to follow someone else instead: her brother. "What the fuck did you do, Micah?" she shouted at her brother's disappearing figure. She ran up to him, giving him the harshest shove she could muster—but he barely flinched. "I will kill you, I swear."

"Leave me alone, Bella," he said venomously. She could have sworn she saw tears brimming in his eyes that night. Maybe she was wrong and it was just the reflection of the waves lapping against the wearing shore, but she took her chances and softened, realizing that there was something about Micah that even she did not know.

"Do you have feelings for her, Micah? Is that it?"

Micah brushed her off, leaving her with Anderson under the faint light of the streetlamps. "They enjoy each other's company,

Bella," Anderson murmured, the extent of what he knew. He hated seeing her like this. There were no words to pacify a frenzied Isabella. Though, in Bella's defense, Anderson's efforts always came close.

"But if he loved her so much, why did he reject her?" I asked, feeling irritated. And then it dawned on me that he was dying. Was he just trying to protect her?

"I don't know, Narns, but Sol took it really hard. One day she told me that she couldn't bear to look at me anymore because I was a carbon copy of him."

"Please don't tell me all of this started because of Micah."

"It was little things, but they added up. Her twin sister disappeared that year. Micah happened and then everything else happened. It took a strain on her. And I guess leaving me was her way of keeping control. But she took Teo, Anderson—she took everyone. And I cared about her so much that I let her."

"Sol Flores," came Mrs. Foti's voice from the front of their classroom.

Isabella twirled her pencil around her fingers, avoiding their teacher's gaze.

"Anyone know where Ms. Flores could be?" Mrs. Foti questioned, her eyes scavenging the classroom for Bella's. The two had always been inseparable, and if there was anybody who would know where Sol was, it was Bella. Her silence spoke incrementally to even their school teacher.

They were twenty four minutes into the period when Sol stormed into the room, gasping for air. "Sorry I'm late," she said. She carried herself with confidence despite the onlookers' peering eyes. And maybe she appeared okay from afar: her lips painted red, her skin slightly aglow from her foundation and her vacant eyes. But the closer she came, the more evident it became that even the strongest concealer could not remedy those sunken eyes, clouded with exhaustion.

"Long night?" Kyle, one of the students, chided.

"You can call it that," she retorted with a smirk.

The class began to snicker, stopping only when met with Mrs. Foti's glaring eyes. What they would never admit is that her behavior shocked all of them. Their seemingly invincible Golden Girl unraveling slowly, falling apart in ways she had once seemed immune to. And time passed, but Sienna's disappearance continued haunting her like the ghost of her lover's past.

And then came the gossip. She heard them when she expected it the least. The townsfolk spoke quietly, their hushed tones betraying them as Sol made out their words. Rumors spread across Holden that Sienna was pregnant with Anderson Flemming's baby and had gone in search of a town where abortion rights were less restrictive. Others speculated that she had fallen victim to a case of demonic possession; the finest exorcists were far away. Some even went on to claim that Sienna was actually dead, she was among the slew of girls abducted by a local killer and her alleged disappearance was a plea of denial on her parents' behalf.

"They bore it together, those days, Anderson, Sol and Teo. It brought them closer together. And it drew us further apart."

And Sol continued stealing shy glances at Micah from afar. She went to see The Nuclear Family play under the pretense of supporting local artists. She stopped by their house every election season to ensure they were registered, stopping only when Micah moved away. If it was his intention to protect her from his cancer, he destroyed her even more by keeping himself at bay.

At his weekly gigs in Cornelia's, she would watch him with an acute intensity that drove him insane. He caught her from the periphery of his eyes. With a vacant face that bore no emotion, he would tilt his head, innocently meeting her gaze.

She would look away.

He savored the scarlet of her cheeks, those diffident eyes and the way her stubborn lips were often pressed in indignation. After all, that was all he had left of her. He could have chosen to have more, but selfishness had never been Micah's vice.

"It was the hardest time of all of our lives."

"And Micah? Didn't he do anything about it?"

"He did tell me he tried to confront her once," she murmured—and he had. On an especially callous December night, he took a detour to Sol's house, wearing his bulky jacket that put her on edge. The feathers from his hood would stick to her clothes. An uncanny coincidence that made it so that whenever Micah wore that jacket, Sol wore velvet. Fucking lint on fucking velvet was a nightmare. It was impossible to get off.

Micah observed her on the other side of her door, covered in velvet. He helped himself in without an invitation—and then he was shouting. He wondered what he was saying. The pleasure of seeing her was so great that he momentarily lost control of his own body. "What are we doing, Sol?" he began, staggering as if her name was his weakness. Nobody had ever said her name like that, not with such passion, intensity and tenderness.

She wondered if he loved her. The words so tempting, she felt them dancing on her tongue. Micah, she would say. Why are you here? Do you love me?

No, he did not love her—but why did that make the least sense of all?

Her words were colder than the day as she parted her lips to say "Is that all?" sweeping Micah into frustration. He would have faltered had he not known her. Micah Henry knew very little about his life then, but Sol—Sol, he knew. He knew that she was better than this. He knew that she was hurting.

"How can you do this to yourself, Sol?"

There he went, saying her name like that again. How could she not forgive him when he was like this?

"I get that I hurt you, but how could you do this to Bella? It was me who hurt you, not her."

Her eyes danced around the room, avoiding his gaze.

"Sol," he implored. "Just make it go away. You love her, don't you?" He was so close to her. "And what about you?" he asked her quietly. "What are you doing, Sol? Going around with those bastards in the team. You're better than this."

He reached for her waist, but she took an abrupt step back, screwing her face into a grimace. "You don't just get to come here and do that, Micah. Do you even know what I've been going through in the last month? You don't know anything."

"I know you."

She scoffed. She wanted to yell—scream even. She wanted to ask him how he dared to say that to her when he had rejected her, providing her with no explanation but rather a series of indecipherable signals. "Leave," she finally said, her voice venomous.

"Sol—"

"Micah Henry," she breathed out, her eyes narrowed into slits. "You heard me. Leave."

He hesitated. There was a simple urge to kiss her senseless. Misery by silence, they were close enough that their lips could touch if he dared. But he sighed, looking away.

Without another word, he made for the door. He hadn't gone back since.

Little did Micah know, Sol looked through the gap on the side of her door at his disappearing figure. When he reached the end of her street, she shut the door despite her reluctance, pressing her back against its wooden frame. Wet, violent tears escaped her eyes. He had left her again without even an ounce of hesitation. It was what he knew best.

But Micah looked back. He really did. He just did it a second after she closed the door, a second too late. He recalculated the venom in her voice, imploring him to leave, and concluded that she was over him. He convinced himself it was for the best.

Bella never knew about this exchange. It was too humiliating for Micah to admit to her that he had gone back. Misery by silence, I tell you. Everyone in this town suffered from it. It wasn't until a few years later that I finally found it all out from him. But we didn't know it then. So Bella and I let ourselves believe that night was the last of the exchanges between the two.

We untangled the last of the fairy lights and asked the townies to help us set them. Bella and I were working around the main square when Anderson's voice stopped me. "Narnie, think you can give me a hand?"

He was balancing three large cardboard boxes, two on each of his hands and one underneath his arm. The third one was beginning to slip. I looked at Bella for approval, but she continued playing with the lights, pretending not to notice him. So I went up to him, sliding the one under his armpit into my arms.

"It's just ornaments for the tree," Anderson said sheepishly. He motioned toward a pine tree in the middle of the square, walking towards it. "You two want to abandon the lights and help me out for a bit?"

Bella already had her mind set: "We're busy."

"Be nice," I said to her when Anderson was far enough.

She rolled her eyes, lowering her voice into a whisper. "He can come and ask me personally."

"He's asking both of us."

"I'm not going."

"You guys coming?" Anderson shouted across the lawn, picking up the last of the ornament boxes to take toward the tree. He looked past me at Bella. "Ella?"

She swallowed, dropping the lights. "I hate you, Anderson Flemming."

Anderson raised an eyebrow.

Flustered, she took a step closer toward him. "I guess I can help."

I tried to hide my excitement as we approached the tree. Teo found us in the middle of the town square, hanging ornaments. Jesus fucking Christ, he mouthed at me, motioning to Anderson and Isabella. The corners of his lips widened into a smile. The moment gave us hope that things could change.

"I saw Nate was in town," Anderson finally said, his voice hollow as he hung a heavy ornament.

Bella reached into the box for an ornament of her own. For a moment, we were all sure she would say nothing. But she didn't, taking us by surprise. "Yeah, he stopped by yesterday," she said. She pulled out an ornament of a naked Santa Claus from one of the boxes. "Wow, seriously? What the hell, Anderson?"

"Mahrsy must have put it in without realizing it."

"Mahrsy?" I asked, glancing between the two.

"Mahrsy," Bella repeated, raising her head to look at him. "How is she?"

"Bigger. She's in kindergarten now."

"Time really flies, doesn't it?"

"She misses you, Bella."

"And who's fault is that?" Bella retorted. At her indignance, I moved closer to Teo, decorating the part of the tree farthest away from the two. An hour later, we were joined by Sol and a couple of townies, who arrived along the curb with another truckload of ornaments. She stole a cheerful glance at Bella and Anderson, who had spent the last hour warming up to each other.

When we were done, we sprawled out on a patch of grass under the tree. Bella heaved out a sigh, stretching her legs before her. "I'm starving."

Anderson brushed the edge of Bella's sneakers with his boots. "Me too."

"You want to order something?" Teo asked them.

Bella nodded.

"What do you want, Bels?"

"I'm not picky."

"We all know that that's not true," Sol said, her voice soft—cautious. "Why don't we order pizza? With chicken and broccoli, the way you like it."

"I'm a vegetarian now," Bella said curtly.

Anderson chuckled, shaking his head. "So much for not being picky, Ella."

"Did you guys know that livestock agriculture produces like, a half of all human caused emissions? And you expect me to eat meat knowing that?"

A dimpled grin spread across Teo's face. He placed his hands on her neck, planting a kiss on her forehead. "We've missed you, Bella."

"So pizza?" she asked him. "We can get olives and tomatoes and—" Her eyes suddenly lit up. "—red peppers! Sol, your favorite."

Sol smiled warily. Maybe she was thinking about how things had ended too fast a year ago. Maybe she was thinking about what she would do differently this time around. But it was useless to think about those days that were wasted in longing because they could no longer be changed. "Okay with me," she said. "Narnie?"

"Pizza sounds good."

"I'll go pick it up then," Teo said, standing up. "Anyone want to come with?"

"I'll go," I said.

He nodded. We placed an order on our way to Carl's pizzaria. When he hung up, he talked about the waste of the months between then and now, about how refreshing it was to have Bella around again, a little like stepping into a nostalgic memory but this time it wasn't just a memory—it was their present.

We arrived at Carl's pizzeria eventually. The bell atop the door jingled as we walked inside, the traffic of the passersby subsiding once we entered its vacant interior. "Ezra," Teo said to the man behind the counter. "What's up, man?"

Ezra's eyes moved toward the source of the noise. "Teo, my man," he greeted. His inquisitive eyes travelled to where I was, lagging behind Teo. A flicker of mischief crossed his eyes. "Nice to see you too, Narnie."

"Just placed an order for three pies," Teo said. "We've been setting up for the holiday festival."

"It'll just be a few more minutes, if you two don't mind."

"I'll be out," Teo said. He removed a pack of cigarettes from his pockets. "Don't let her pay, Ezra."

I walked closer to the counter as Teo left with a jingle behind him. "Long morning?"

"Something like that."

I rested my elbows on the counter, burying my cheeks in my palms. "You won't believe who Bella's in town with right now."

"Oh yeah?"

"Anderson. And Sol."

"How did that happen?"

"We were all setting up the holiday decorations and Anderson called me over and I was with Bella so she came over with and—uh, and yeah."

He laughed, tending to the oven. "It seems like you're having a good morning. The pizzas are almost ready. Do you want me to make us coffee?"

I looked outside the glass door at Teo. "But the others—"

"Just one cup?"

"Okay. Just one."

I wondered if his coffee had confessional properties—because the conversation somehow went to his father. "I went to visit him yesterday. After you left, you know? And we talked. He told me he can't even tell the days passing him by. One—thirty, it's all a blur. That it's like a long, unending day where the darkness never ends." I asked him to pour me another cup of coffee, but all I wanted was an infinite serving of him.

He was a supernova, burning in silence. I placed my hand on his and let myself believe I could get by with a minor burn—but he was a supernova, billions of kelvins of exploding heat. I was bound to an excruciating end.

I immersed myself in him anyway, listening quietly until the bell atop the door jingled once again. I expected to see Teo, but Ezra's pretty eyed lady walked in, a woolen scarf covering everything except for her eyes. Ezra beamed a little more than he should have, his face gathering vigor. "Larisa."

I became ash.

"The town is so full today, Ez," she said, sliding her scarf off her face. "I'm exhausted. Can you make me a latte?"

I slid my mug across the counter. "The pizzas are probably getting cold."

"Oh," Larisa said, noticing me for the first time. "Hi."

I reached into my pocket for my debit card, but he stopped me. "Teo said not to let you pay."

"Well, somebody has to pay."

"It's on me, Narns," he said. He stacked three boxes of pizza on top of one another. "You think you can handle it?"

I nodded, sliding it into my arms. "Thanks, Ezra."

Teo and I returned to the town center to find Bella sniffling uncontrollably. "So everything is okay between us?" she was saying.

Anderson wrapped his arms around her, resting his chin on top of her head. "Everything is going to be okay, Bella."

Her tentative eyes met Sol's. "And Micah?"

"I'll talk to him," Sol said. "Fix things again, maybe, if that's what he wants."

"And if he doesn't?"

"We'll get started plotting his murder," Anderson said.

Bella smiled at her once best friend. "Deal."

I dropped the pizzas in front of them. "We come bearing goods."

"Took you two long enough," Sol said, opening one of the boxes.

"Narnie was taking her time with Parker in there," Teo said in his defense. "So blame her. Not me."

Bella grabbed a slice of pizza. "All forgiven."

"What's the deal with you two, anyway?" Sol asked me. "Not to pry or anything, but you were getting pretty cosy in the rink."

"That was nothing."

"It didn't look like nothing."

"He's in love with somebody else."

"Is that a joke?"

"Why don't you ask him yourself? Ask him about his pretty eyed lady."

"His what now?"

I grabbed a pizza, plopping down on the grass next to Bella. "I don't want to talk about it."

"Okay, just to be clear, do we hate Ezra now?" Anderson asked sincerely.

Sol dropped her crust into the box. "She's just being thick, Andy."

"Wait, did he actually use the words pretty eyed lady to describe a girl other than you?" Bella asked. "Because if he did, that's fucked up and we hate him."

"We hate him!" Sol declared.

"Don't encourage this, Sol," Teo said. "Listen, Narns, if you're hurt about something he did, you should talk to him, you know? Don't let it fester."

But I let it fester. Of course I let it fester. I let it fester until five days later, when I finally mustered the courage to visit him in his caravan. I plucked a flower from the ground as I went up his door, where I paused to reconsider. Why was I here? Everyone else was in town, Sol, Teo and Anderson by the harbor on a Friday night. And maybe Bella was with Micah, laughing at one of his ridiculous jokes.

I swallowed, fighting a growing lump in my throat. Ezra, I would say. Who is she to you?

No. Too confrontational.

"Ezra, I like you, and I think we should date," I considered saying.

Absolutely not.

I racked my head for something that wouldn't scare him away. But before I could reach for the door again, I was being pushed against its thin fibreglass frame and gently turned around. My body relented to the force of my intruder as I was met with his eyes. Without another word, Ezra snaked his arms around my waist and buried his face in my neck.

What was he doing, Ezra Parker? He opened the door and guided us inside, his eyes not once leaving mine.

He dropped his keys on the dining table and I faltered, struggling between keeping him close and pushing him away. He brought his hands to my neck. "What's the matter?"

I pulled away from him, sitting on the edge of his bed. My thoughts wandered to Larisa again. I wondered how he could do this to me. How could he toy with me knowing that she was still in love with another girl?

He went on his knees, levelling his head with mine. "Talk to me, Narnie."

I averted my gaze from his. "I found your poem."

"Poem?"

"The one you lost back in October. You know, about Larisa."

He placed his hands on my chin and forced me to look at him. "Is that it?"

"What do you mean, is that it? I know you still have feelings for her."

"And did you ever think to consult me about my own feelings?" he asked. I looked away, causing him to sigh. "You're being silly."

Pretty eyed lady, he had written. A sinner, my muse. And after yesterday, after he abandoned me for her, did he expect me to just believe him?

"She was my pretty eyed lady, Narnie," he finally said, dropping his hands. "But that was all she ever was. Now I've found someone else, someone I adore so much more."

I released the breath I had been holding and looked at him again. "Really?"

"Really."

"Who?"

"Who do you think?"

"Me?"

"You."

"Really?"

"Narnie," he groaned. "I'm on edge here, waiting for you to let me kiss you."

"Where's my incentive?"

"Oh, you need an incentive now?"

"Yes."

"How about your incentive is that you're crazy about me?"

"I'm not though."

He raised an eyebrow. "Is that so?

"Yeah."

"Okay then," he said with a chuckle. He began to get up, but I stopped him.

"I'm just kidding."

He looked at me, his eyes calculating my next move. It was my greatest act of bravery, pressing my lips to his. All of my worries evaporated into nothingness with that one touch. And I relived our story all over again, from that first day by Mrs. Liebson's desk to the shy glances we exchanged in the weeks that came. To our fleeting drives along Holden's high altitude roads, to his sorrows—to his nostalgia. He tasted like strawberries.

Maybe I was too young to know what love was. And maybe one day I would look back at this very moment and laugh at my youthful naivety, warning my daughter about boys like Ezra Parker, who stole your heart at seventeen without your permission and never gave it back.

But I could hear his heart, merely an inch away, beating steadfast, and I suddenly knew; I knew that his heart was beating for this very moment. So I let go of my restraints and latched onto that moment as if we were approaching the end of the world. And maybe we were. But nothing else seemed to matter as I threw care to the wind and kissed him again and again until we drowned in the heart of that invincible winter night.

CHAPTER 10

Ezra's bedroom smelled like him on Monday mornings. I engulfed myself in it when I couldn't engulf myself in him. In the evenings after cheerleading practice, when I was procrastinating on homework and college applications, I went through his books. One particular evening, I came across Siddhartha again. Clara's copy. Thoughts of Edem raced back into my head—and all I could think about as Ezra cooked us ramen was how we needed to see Micah again.

We ate in silence, Ezra finishing up his missed assignments as I finished my soup. The last thing I expected was for the door to suddenly fling open with a pair of familiar eyes exhausting my vision.

"Am I interrupting something?" he said, inviting himself in. The door shut behind him with a thud. He bought in with himself a distinct, palpable urgency that was uncharacteristic of him.

Ezra lifted his head toward the door, heaving out a sigh.

The visitor's eyes traveled from Ezra to me. "Moved on just as quickly I see."

"Don't, Alex."

"When I saw her, I knew it was just a matter of time."

"For fuck's sake—"

"These things, Ezra—they just happen, don't they?"

"That's not the same."

"Or maybe they don't. Unless," Alex paused, his eyes meeting mine. "You're just using lovely over here to get over Larisa."

Ezra released another sigh. "Why are you here, Alex?"

"I have news."

"News?"

"About Clara."

Ezra stood up from the table.

"Sometime soon," he continued. "I'll be back."

With a fleeting acknowledgement in my direction, he left through the door he had come from. I turned to face Ezra, finding his face laced with curiosity and sorrow.

"Ezra," I breathed out, rushing up to him. "Are you okay?"

I flinched as he brushed me away.

"Clara thought she was going to marry Alex one day," he said later that night. We were lying under his covers because of the cold. "But after she disappeared, it took that shitbag less than two months to move on. With Larisa."

I sunk into his chest, wondering how people could move on just like that. One day lovers and the next day strangers. Didn't nostalgia catch up to them?

"Is that why you hate him so much?"

"Forget grief, it took him a second to move on. How do people like that claim to knowing how to love?"

"He's not like you, Ezra. He doesn't matter."

He brought his hands to mine, engulfing my tiny fingers into his. "Whatever happens to us, I'll never do you wrong like that, Narns."

What did I do to deserve him? All I ever knew was loss.

"I hope I never lose you," I said quietly. I thought about Papa and found my heart turning hollow again. "If I didn't have you, I would feel so lonely."

"Why do you think I surround myself with books all the time?"

I moved my head to his pillow, facing him. "To forget for a moment that you are alone?"

He smiled weakly, bumping my nose with his. The tender gesture flooded my body with warmth. It was hard to imagine, in those moments, that what we had was not infinite. It was hard to foresee the cruelty that awaited us ahead.

"What about you?" he said. "You know so much about me. What do I know about you?"

"You know about me."

"Barely."

"Well, what do you want to know?"

"Do you ever think about your father?"

I felt my throat constrict. His eyes flickered with worry, as if he was entertaining the thought that he had miscalculated. Nobody had ever looked at me like that before, with such an urgency, like they wanted nothing more than to devour my sadness and transform it into their own.

"I miss his rhubarb pie," I finally said.

He brought his hands to my neck, stroking it gently. "What happened to him?"

I succumbed into his touch, my mind flooding with thoughts of Papa. His hands lingered in the seconds that went by, like they would never again come undone. An icy breeze seeped in through the crevices of his door. It was suddenly so cold that I could shiver, but even with arms ridden with goosebumps, I felt warm in his embrace. And maybe I was ready, finally, to think about that day without feeling like it would destroy me.

I was born prematurely to Theodore and Maya Larson in Wood-haven Hospital on a cloudless Spring day. "It was the best day of my life," Papa would say during our family gatherings—our fragmented family gatherings, consisting of his large American family, his prideful eyes and the way he would pull Mama into him in between conversations, thanking her for delighting him with the pleasure of being his.

And we never spoke about it: our fragmented family dinners. We never spoke about Maya Larson's family, why I had never met them or why she acted as if they were dead to her. It became more apparent throughout the years that it was because they had disowned her for falling in love with a man outside of her race—or maybe she had disowned them, for it was hardly a sin to fall in love.

I went by for the first seventeen years of my life without as little as a single indication into her past life—and Papa's family, they had certainly taken her in as their own. And so I never experienced a loss of a family. How can you experience the loss of something that was never yours?

It happened early in the morning one Friday, on the first day of August. Mama and Papa were loading tents into our car when it came: a phone call, three rings and suddenly an unknown voice on the other end of the line, asking for Maya.

I pressed the phone to my ears. "Hello, who is this?"

"Maya?"

"Can I ask who is calling?"

"Can I speak to Maya?" the stranger requested, his voice shaky in an attempt to conceal his heavy accent. "Maya Rai?"

I pressed the phone to my chest, wondering why he had taken her by her maiden name, a name that emerged only on rare occasions. "Mam, there's someone on the phone for you!"

She walked in through the front door. "Who is it baby?"

"They're asking for Maya, Maya Rai?"

Her eyes slightly widening, she took the phone from my hands. And I found her crying on the rest stop on our way to Bluestone Camp later that day. And then came the arguments, late at night, when Mama and Papa suspected I was fast asleep, their voices faint against the backdrop of our noisy city.

"We're going, Maya," Papa would say, his voice firm and uncompromising.

"We are not going, Theodore."

"Ishan said it himself. Your father is dying."

"Let him."

"Maya, please. Now is not the time to be stubborn."

"How can I ever forgive them, Theodore? They punished me for falling in love with you. They are dead to me."

And she sobbed. She sobbed when she thought I couldn't hear. She sobbed until her tears ran dry. And she sobbed as Papa booked a one way ticket to Kathmandu, promising her that he would come back only after making things right with her family. And it was then that another call came, a call just as treacherous, but this one from the American embassy.

"There was a bombing in Atatürk during Theodore Larson's layover."

"A suicide bomber, our intelligence agencies say."

"He wasn't able to board his connecting flight to Kathmandu that day."

"That is how Papa left us," I said hoarsely. "He left us with possibility and an arresting sense of what could have been. He left us trying to make things right. He left us with nothing except his rhubarb pie."

"Narnie," Ezra said, as if he would do anything he could to take my pain away.

"It's okay. I'm over it," I assured—but could anyone truly recover from such a thing? I closed my eyes and saw in the darkness Theodore Larson's green eyes. I opened my lips and tasted in between my words the sweetness of fresh rhubarb.

"Who are you trying to fool, Narnie Larson?" Ezra asked me, tearing me away from my thoughts.

I faltered.

"You don't have to pretend you're not hurting. You're so good at that. Why are you so good at that?"

"I don't mean to," I began. I closed my eyes again. It had been months since I last allowed myself to cry. Did that make me a bad person? At this thought, I couldn't help but feel my eyes water. Those first days had been so painful—so much so that I had numbed myself to the grief before I could fully process it. Had I deprived Papa of the mourning he deserved because of that? Was he looking down on me tonight, condemning me for my apathy? Was he ashamed of the person I had become? I couldn't breathe.

"Narnie," Ezra began softly, his fingers brushing against my cheeks. "Narnie, fuck, I didn't mean to hurt you."

But it was too late. I couldn't stop the torrent of tears coursing down my cheeks, longing for Papa's comfort. Ezra smothered my face in his chest, his fingers gently massaging my head. And I cried. I cried as if I had discovered what it was for the very first time. I cried like I couldn't get enough. I cried as if my tears would elicit divine intervention—as if that intervention could bring Papa back. I cried at the thought of his body, so still against his casket that day in mid August—how peaceful he had looked then, how even in death, he seemed to say, Narnie, my baby girl, our story does not have to end with death. It will begin again one day, you hear me? And I will be waiting for you until then. That is my promise.

CHAPTER 11

Lost in the amber of our moments, we told ourselves that the truth could wait until the end of the holiday season. We wanted nothing more than to forget, even if for a fleeting day or two, that we were not living in a town plagued by Edem Whittaker's vices.

I thought about taking Ezra home for our holiday dinner, teasing him with the possibility of it when we were supposed to be revising each other's essays in Pierre-Louis' eight a.m. His eyes brightened all at once. "I'll be there, Narnie."

It hurt to see how much he missed his family. He spent the remainder of class going through photo albums on his laptop, pretending he was taking notes.

He arrived at the door at seven holding a gift bag. Inside it, Nana found a book of poetry by Geoffrey Chaucer, who by a kind twist of fate was her favorite author.

"You didn't have to, Ezra," she said modestly.

"It's my pleasure, Ms. Larson."

"Call me Sofia," she said. She scanned the book as he hung his jacket on the coat hanger by our door.

He treaded towards the kitchen, where I was. "It smells so lovely, Sofia."

"Don't praise me. Praise Narnie. She made salmon teriyaki."

"I haven't had salmon teriyaki since last May," he said quietly. Since last May, when his mother had passed away. I let the topic dwindle.

Nana placed Ezra's gift by the fireplace and led him to the dining room, where the table had been set for three. Where I had set a plate for Mama, it was no longer there. I glanced at Nana, seeing that her eyes were already on me. "Mama isn't joining us?"

A weak smile overtook her face. "In her office."

I ignored my frustration as we sat down. How lucky was I, that along with a dead father, I had to reckon with an absent mother? Ezra must have noticed my frustration because he slipped his hand onto my thigh, squeezing it.

"We moved to Holden during the war, you know," Nana said as we began eating. "One of the main tenets of the local religion was its rejection of war. The abbot had always been very powerful. He made sure everyone who lived in the district and abided by the religion was exempt from the draft. Your grandfather and I came because we didn't know how long it would last. We wanted to protect our kids.

"Some people saw it as unjust, but he upheld the exemption using the first amendment. And people eventually gave up with justice the way they always do and began seeing it as an opportunity to save themselves. No one wanted to go to Vietnam. So Holden became more and more occupied. I remember, at the peak of the war, it was the most expensive district in the country."

"It's a little tragic," Ezra said. "How the only ones who could save themselves were the ones with money."

Nana nodded wistfully. "Yes, dear, we were very fortunate."

"Is there a reason you didn't go back to San City? You know, after the war?"

"We fell in love with the place—with its rolling hills, its rich culture. It reminded Terrace, my husband, of our honeymoon in Slovenia. It's a beautiful place, isn't it?"

"It really is."

I smiled. Mr. Ezra Parker, who wanted nothing more than to get the hell out of this town, agreeing that it was a beautiful place? I would never let him live that one down.

As I finished my dinner to a conversation between my favorite people in the world, the feeling crept up on me again that I was a part of a family. I told myself that the only person who could complete this table was Mama—and Papa, if he was still here—but maybe it was time for me to accept that he was gone. Or that he had never left. And maybe he never would, not as long as he was alive in my memory.

At the end of the night, Ezra helped Nana load the dishes in the dishwasher. I cleared the table, preparing a plate for Mama as the two continued their discussion on the town's history. I was putting away the last of the containers when my phone beeped with a notification from Bella. A bunch of us are in town for the holiday festival. come with? ooo, bring blankets!

"Bella wants us to meet her in town for the holiday festival," I said, catching the two by surprise.

"The holiday festival," Nana said reflectively. "Is that today?"

"Yeah, according to Bella."

"I didn't even notice. Oh, how time flies."

Ezra dried the first of the pots. "We can't just leave in the middle of this, Narns."

"No, no!" Nana exclaimed. "You two go. I'll take it from here."

"Let me help you finish up, at least."

Tears welled in my eyes as he dried the rest of the dishes. I am in love with you, Ezra Parker, I wanted to shout. Instead, I took the opportunity to change into warmer clothes while waiting for him to finish up. The distant sound of Nana's laughter overcame our once silent home. I wondered how everything could happen so fast, how grief could so easily succumb to love's embrace. Sliding into my clothes, I teased myself with the thought that maybe we were not condemned to misery. Maybe something beautiful lay ahead. Maybe there was a possibility for us after all.

I drove us into town. We belted Pinkish Sunrise at the top of our lungs on the way there.

"We come bearing blankets," I said as I spotted Bella, Anderson, Sienna, Micah, Sol and Mateo. They were sprawled around a bonfire, roasting marshmallows and drinking out of Hydro Flasks and thermoses. I occupied the empty space next to Micah, forcing him to scoot closer to Sol.

"Took you two long enough," Bella said with a sigh.

"Looking cosy, Bel-Bel," Ezra teased, seeing how close she was to Anderson.

Bella blushed, saying nothing.

"Micah made us build the pit," Sol chided, rolling her eyes. "Like, from scratch."

"Well, the fire had to go somewhere, Sol," Micah said pointedly.

"I'm not complaining. My Instagram story is on point."

"That's all she cares about..."

"Excuse me?"

"You heard me."

"Oh my god," Sienna groaned. "If you two don't shut up."

Bella gave Ezra and I cushions for the floor. "We were just playing Never Have I Ever," she explained sheepishly. "Blanket, Ezra?"

Ezra handed out the blankets we had strung along, first to Bella and then to everyone else.

"Bella made hot chocolate," Sol said, distributing a thermos from across the circle. "We saved a batch for you two."

Ezra took the thermos from her, releasing a happy breath. "Bella, our goddess."

I motioned for Ezra to unscrew the lid. He chuckled, shaking his head as he poured me a cup. "So this is really how we're choosing to go into the holidays, huh?"

"If by that you mean going into the holidays with a bang, then yes," Anderson said with a laugh.

I raised an eyebrow at him. "Is the hot chocolate that good?"

Sol bit her lip. "Give it to her already, Ezra."

I took the lid from Ezra. "Oh," I said as the distinct smell of cinnamon whiskey wafted up my nose. "I see." I narrowed my eyes at Sol. "Whore, you promised me hot chocolate."

"Can't go into the holidays without Fireball."

"Why is it in thermoses anyway?"

"Well," Anderson began. "If we don't count the fact that most of us underage and drinking on government property, Mrs. Henry keeps looking at us."

"Yeah, Bella," Sienna began, narrowing her eyes at Bella. "What's up with that?"

Micah glanced at us wearily. His illness, of course. After countless nights in the hospital, Mrs. Henry was hanging by a thread. And it showed in the strained smiles she projected to others between her fearful, intermittent glances at Micah.

Bella shrugged. "She's just protective."

"Mrs. Henry's like that," Sol said softly, rising to Bella's defense.

Sienna readjusted her blanket, looking at her sister. "Okay, can we continue now? Teo was up." When nobody said anything, her eyes deflected between Anderson and Bella. She cast them back down, releasing a sigh. "Teo?"

"Uh, never have I ever gone skinny dipping in broad daylight."

"Alright. Pass it over," Sol said, referring to Teo's thermos. She and Micah exchanged wistful glances, suppressing a smile. I wondered if things were okay with them again. Would they look as free as they did if they weren't? Or were they just going through the motions of nostalgia again, the way they always did?

As they took a sip of their drink, Bella looked between the two. "You two went skinny dipping? Together? Seriously? Sol, you saw him with his guy out?"

Anderson and I burst out in laughter. "What the fuck is his guy, Bella?" I said, looking at her.

"Don't talk to me, Narnie."

"When?" Teo asked hesitantly.

Micah met Sol's eyes. "The spring before I left. Right?"

"Yeah," she barely whispered out.

"That is disgusting," Bella muttered, shaking her head in disapproval. "Disgusting, disgusting."

Sienna motioned toward her sister. "Sol, your turn."

"Um," Sol drawled. Her cheeks suddenly reddened—and I doubted it was just because of the cold. "Never have I ever purposely hurt someone I love."

Micah took another sip of his whiskey.

"Who did you hurt, Micah?" Sol asked quietly.

He indulged her gaze. "Don't try to get all emotional on me now, Flores."

"I wasn't—"

"I'm not drunk enough for this," Sienna said, taking a sip of her cup.

"Let's move on!" Bella said quickly. "Micah?"

He scratched the side of his brow. "Never Have I Ever□ broken the law."

Sienna rolled her eyes, taking a shot. "Okay boomer."

Ezra, Bella, Anderson and Teo grabbed their thermoses as well. I shook my head at them. "You criminals. What have you done?"

"Pot, arson—nothing too crazy," Bella dismissed. "And fyi, you two should be drinking." Her eyes shifted between Sol and I. "Underage drinking, hello?"

"Guilty as charged," Sol said, taking a thermos. She suddenly put it down, narrowing her eyes at Micah. "Oh my god, you boozer. You've broken the law."

Micah chuckled. "I forgot underage drinking is a crime."

"Not to mention every other shitty thing you did when you were eighteen."

"Easy, Solita."

"Your Never Have I Ever is invalid."

"You guys talk too much," Sienna groaned. "Like, your girl just wants to get drunk."

"Okay then, Narnie, you go," Teo said.

I bit my lip. "Never have I ever had a one night stand."

Anderson, Micah and Sol took a sip. Predictable. But then I saw Ezra reaching for his thermos. My heart panged with jealousy. How many? I wanted to ask. I let silence follow.

Just then, Alex and Larisa approached our bonfire, clad in heavy winter jackets. Micah exchanged a handshake with Alex. "Glad you showed up, man," he said. "Who's the pretty lady?"

I narrowed my eyes at Larisa as Alex said, "This is Larisa. Larisa, Micah."

"Hi Micah," she said. She sat next to Sol, directly across Ezra and I, making my body flare with contempt. "Good to see you too, Ezra. And you, Narnie. It's good to see you."

Who did she think she was, showing up uninvited and pretending she knew me?

"You too," I said, but my voice wavered.

Sensing my indignation, Sol raised an eyebrow. Everything okay? she mouthed.

I rolled my eyes and motioned toward Larisa. Ezra's ex.

Her lips formed an o.

"We were just playing Never Have I Ever," Sienna explained. "Join us?"

"Of course," Larisa said. She sat down, Alex following behind her. "Who's up?"

"Sienna," Teo said.

"Never have I ever been in love," Sienna said.

Everyone passed their bottles around for a drink. Larisa heaved a thermos to her lips, her eyes momentarily scavenging for Ezra's. As they converged, a melancholy smile marred his face. I hated that she still affected him like this, that she had the ability to undo everything I did to make him happy with a simple glance. He entertained her shy gaze—or maybe it was all in my head; maybe this madness was just the byproduct of falling in love.

"Never been in love, Narnie?" Anderson said, raising an eyebrow. "Interesting."

Ezra nudged my shoulder. "I guess we'll just have to change that, won't we?"

"If you're up for the challenge," I said curtly.

"Don't doubt me already, Narnie."

"I don't doubt you."

He placed his hand on my neck, forcing me to look at him. "You better not."

"Never have I ever gotten over my first love," Micah was saying.

"Micah, it's not your turn," Sol said quietly. She brought her fingers to his thermos in an effort to strip it away. It was clear that the alcohol was slipping into his bloodstreams, slowly clouding his judgement.

A pithy frown settled on Micah's face, causing her to loosen her grasp. "Never have I ever regretted anything more than that crazy girl," he continued.

She sighed. She would not admit that the gentle motion of his eyes scavenging for hers delighted her beyond explanation. Or that for the fleeting moment that they waged warfare with their eyes, the animosity they had mustered for each other faded into nothing—and they almost became one.

He leaned closer to her, leaving a trail of fumes with his words. "Never have I ever had a reason to believe in love before her."

"Never have I ever," she began, her cheeks rosy from his close proximity.

"It's not your turn, Solita," he interjected with a lopsided smile.

"Guys, if you're done," Anderson said bluntly. "We'd like to continue."

Sol inched away from him. The idea of almost is a painful one. Sol and Micah were almost everything they wanted to be.

"You okay, Sol?" Teo asked, noticing the sudden shift in her aura.

She cleared her throat. "Hey, can I actually talk to you for a moment? Excuse us."

Teo nodded, letting her sweep him away from the circle.

An unsettling silence struck us in the moment that came, settling in the vicinity like an unwanted presence.

"Someone's still not over someone," Sienna finally said, avoiding Micah's gaze.

"Oh boy," Anderson muttered. "Drink up."

I sighed. Under the blanket, Ezra took my hand into his.

"Ezra..."

He closed the gap between us, chuckling into my lips. "No need to say anything."

When we pulled away, six pairs of eyes were on us.

"So, you and Narnie, huh?" Larisa said to Ezra as he dropped my hand and grabbed a marshmallow and a nearby skewer.

"Yeah," he said slowly. He looked at my face for permission. When I smiled, he gently nudged my chin with his knuckles. "She's my girl."

All at once, December's wrath faded into something kinder—warmer. My heart fluttered blissfully in my chest.

"About time," Bella said, rolling her eyes. "It's not like this hasn't been in the makings for the last five months."

I turned to look at him again, my jacket ricocheting his. How did I get so lucky?

Teo came back to our circle then. "Sol had to leave," he explained sheepishly, rubbing the back of his neck. Micah's eyes darted toward him in a subconscious reflex. She was supposed to be there. Had he made her leave?

"No thanks to you, Micah," Bella said, narrowing her eyes at him.

"Bella, please."

"I don't know why you always make things so complicated. You did it then and you're doing it again."

Anderson cleared his throat. "Guys."

"Why the fuck don't you just tell her you have feelings for her?"

A wisp of wind slid in through my scarf, eliciting goosebumps.

"Maybe we should do karaoke," Sienna said warily. "You up for it, Micah?"

He chuckled to hide his dejection. "I don't play anymore."

"Oh please. I bet the talent's still there."

"I'm going home," Bella declared. She haphazardly gathered her belongings. We were all too tipsy to react empathetically—and Bella, she was determined. Just when we were all sure she was going to leave us for the night, Anderson grabbed her wrist, pulling her unsuspecting body toward his. She fell onto his lap.

"We're not doing this," he said angrily. "Not this time."

She relented, her cheeks reddening with embarrassment.

"I'll go," Micah said, releasing a sigh. "I'll find her."

But he never did find her that night. According to a text Bella sent me at two in the morning, he didn't find his way home either. We speculated where he could have been for hours. Mrs. Henry eventually found him at seven, sprawled out with frostbites on Lorimer Avenue. Sol was driving past their house when she saw Bella sobbing into her phone, telling me how Micah had been hospitalized again. What a curse that he had to return, just when he seemed to be getting better.

The next succession of events unraveled nightmarishly for all of us, but especially for Sol. She had barely reached the Henrys' driveway when Bella's shaky words debilitated her: "Micah's in the hospital if you want to see him."

It was Bella's greatest act of submission, telling Sol about Micah. Any sane person would have stuck around to see that she was okay, but Sol spun in an urgent resolve back to her car. It rained violently on her way to the hospital. She aggressively navigated the rush hour traffic in an attempt to race through time. Her heart heavy against her chest, she found her body sweltering despite the chilly weather. Her every symptom suggested that she was on the verge of a heart attack.

Micah was on the brink of sleep when the hospital door swung open and her breathless figure revealed herself to him. He smiled warmly, an attempt to be charming, I suppose, but his weakness betrayed him, revealing his exhaustion.

"You really don't care about me, do you, Micah?" she said in a wisp of breath.

"Sol—"

She walked in, closing the door behind her. "No. No Sol."

He pressed his lips together as he attempted to make sense of the chaos enveloping his mind. Her sunken eyes flickered with defeat, like she was finally giving up on him. She was exhausted because god, loving this man was exhausting. Micah wanted nothing more than to abandon his convictions and engulf her in his arms. But they stood in silence, unspoken words hanging on the tip of their tongues.

"Help me, Micah," she finally said, her voice barely above a whisper. "Tell me what's going on with you. Tell me what you're thinking and why I have this feeling in my heart that you love me even when you keep telling me you don't. And don't tell me that it's complicated because I know it's not. If we can't be anything, can we at least be friends?"

"We can't be friends, Sol," he said softly. "In which universe can you and I be friends?"

"We can try."

"There. I'm trying. And I don't think I can continue."

"Why?"

Because I'm crazy about you, he wanted to say.

"Why Micah?"

"Because..."

"Because what?"

"Because—"

"Because?"

Micah looked away from her. "Because nothing."

Her knees slackened. Misery by silence, I tell you. "I'll get out of here," she said at last. "I'll send you flowers and a cheap get well soon card. I won't care anymore. I swear I won't." But she cared—she so obviously did. She prepared then to turn on her heel and leave for good, but Micah's mellow voice overcame the hospital room, entrapping her.

"I have cancer."

She forgot how to breathe.

CHAPTER 12

When I went to visit Micah that morning, I found Sol on one of those dreadful chairs in the hospital corridor. She sat motionlessly on its faded synthetic surface, her eyes red from crying. "Micah's been moved to the ICU," she said hoarsely. He was there for the next seven days, into the New Year.

We spent New Year's Eve on Nana's roof, all of us. Our bodies hollow from mourning and our eyes damp with tears, we tried to pretend that death was not the end. But Micah's absence was a haunting reminder that life was not as stubborn as we had believed. It could have been any one of us in that emergency room—it could have been Bella.

I looked at Ezra, who had excused himself to the very edge of the roof. He was smoking a cigarette, its fumes pirouetting before him before vanishing into the thin December air. He looked so at peace with himself, sitting on that silver bed of concrete. He eventually finished the cigarette, his silence pacifying the violet night.

"What are you thinking about?" I asked, taking a seat next to him.

He crushed the butt of his cigarette on the floor. "Just thinking about Micah."

"What about Micah?"

"Well, you know," he began softly. "If he's going to be okay. What we're going to do if something happens to him. If he doesn't—you know—make it."

"Who said Micah isn't going to make it?"

"Micah did."

"Well, Micah's biased. He doesn't know any better."

He sighed, his eyes meeting mine. They found mine so wistfully, like they were looking at someone other than me, someone that he, by the radical abandonment of all caution and control, had developed a little more fondness than he had bargained for.

"Stop looking at me like that," I mustered through my racing heart.

He firmly shook his head, caressing my cheeks with his fingers. "Let me." I smoldered under his touch, my every rational thought withering away. As his fingertips grazed my lips, I closed my eyes, pretending this moment was as unending as the night felt, unraveling at her slow, sedating pace. "You're beautiful," he murmured.

I opened my eyes again to find his nose caressing mine. He planted a fleeting kiss there before pulling away. "Maybe you're right. Maybe we'll get a miracle."

"Maybe."

"On that thought," he digressed. He reached into his pocket, removing a piece of paper that was dilapidated on its edges, one that at first glance seemed to have been through a whirlwind of adversaries. "I have something for you." He motioned towards his lap, the corners of his lips moving ever so slightly, insinuating a smile. "Read it with me?"

I raised an eyebrow, sliding onto his lap—and once again I felt his warm skin pressed against my own, obstructed by just a layer of clothing. His dizzying touch penetrating my thin jacket, he snaked his arms around mine, positioning the paper before me. "I started it when I first saw you. Like really saw you, you know? That day in the field. You were reading Siddhartha."

I felt my sanity shredding into pieces.

"Let's see," he murmured, resting his chin on my shoulder. "Start there, at Don't."

My eyes fell to the paper. Did I know then that I was assembling the labyrinth of my own doom? We never do—not at seventeen.

"Don't look so exhausted, darling," I began softly. "As if you have been strung by a lifetime of hardship, as if your existence can be depicted as nothing more than the purplish bruise on a severed knuckle, as if you have only endured lovers who pulled away a little too quickly, those who did not savor every fiber of your being, your quirks and your inconsistencies, only to desire you again when there was no more to you..."

"As if there could be no more to you," he murmured, trailing his hands down my arms, leaving a pathway of goosebumps at their wake. "How can I capture your essence without being at a loss—without falling short of the words that feel futile in this attempt to express what you are beginning to mean to me?

"How dare I call myself a poet when I can spend a lifetime writing poetry and eternities thereafter, only to crumble at the realization that I had never done you justice—that I never could?

"Don't look so exhausted, darling. Just let me be, just this once, the voice to comfort your darkest days, the balm to remedy your wounds. It is the least I can do."

I was on the verge of tears when he finished, my heart fluttering like a madwoman who had found her home at last. I took his hand into my palm, soft despite their many adventures. "You know, declarations of love usually come before you tell the world I'm your girl."

"I guess I never quite had the chance to formally ask you."

"Ask me what?"

"You know what."

"Nope."

"Narnie, baby."

I felt my heart catapult again. Baby? Had he just called me baby? How could I even begin to tell him what that did to me? My restless mind. This weariness that I felt so viciously in my bones, torn between euphoria and terror. I could never tell him, not even if I wanted to. It was a mission of futility.

When I turned around, I found our faces so close in proximity that his breath dangerously caressed my lips: it was a whisper of a touch, the sensation so fickle that I wondered if he was there at all. "Yeah?" I whispered. His impenetrable body pressed into mine as our lips coalesced for a kiss, his fingers scavenging for my neck. In the distant skies, fireworks exploded. Reverberations followed in my heart.

He reached for a blanket and encased himself in it, blanketing me with him. Suspended in the ember of that moment, I was madly and irrevocably in love with Ezra Parker. And I wanted to shout it despite knowing that its depth would be lost in translation. And maybe that was the greatest condemnation of this existence. We were put in this world to reckon with love, but neglected as we feverishly scavenged for ways to prove it.

We woke up the next morning to the bluest skies. He was staring at them longingly from my windowsill. "Morning."

I extended my arms in a stretch, releasing a yawn. "Morning."

"Had to move down here on Maya's command. Everyone left a little after you fell asleep."

"Did Mama give you a hard time?"

"Not at all."

"Good."

"I wanted to wait until you woke up to go," he continued sheepishly. "I have a shift at Carl's."

I tried to hide my disappointment as he met my eye. "On New Year's day?"

He smiled, walking up to me. "No need to be so sad."

"Leave me then, Mr. Parker."

He placed a fleeting kiss on my forehead. "I'll call you."

"If you must."

He helped me make my bed before leaving through the front door. And I was surprised to find him on the other side of the door a few minutes later, the doorbell ringing to signal his presence. With cheeks crimson from the cold, he rubbed the back of his neck. "I think I left my wallet in your room," he said—and he had. He returned holding his wallet on one hand and his phone on the other.

He apologized before leaving—and the doorbell rang again. "What now, Ezra?"

He mischievously leaned into me, pressing his cold lips onto mine. "Forgot that."

I laughed as he pulled away. I watched him get on his motorbike, hoping that he would conjure another excuse to come back. But our vicinity sounded with the familiar cacophony of his Harley drifting away. I bashfully closed the door once again. When the doorbell rang again a few minutes later, I opened it quickly. "What did you forget this time?" I teased, my fingers toying with the surface of the doorknob. When I raised my head to discover a pair of frenzied blue eyes, I took a step backward. "Alex."

He took one step closer. "It's Ezra," he said, holding up an envelope. "We need to talk."

<h1 style="text-align:center">CHAPTER 13</h1>

"How do I know I can trust you?" I breathed out, my grasp on the doorknob tightening. A callous breeze swept in through the barely open door, enveloping me in its cold. It was difficult to pinpoint just what was more unsettling: the possibility of Ezra being in danger or Alex being the one to deliver the news.

"Come on, Narnie," he pressed, his face stringing with concern. "Have I ever done anything to wrong you?"

"No, but—"

"I get it," he continued. "You're just being loyal to him. He told you that I betrayed Lara like he always does. Some sob story about how I moved on with Larisa without grieving for her. I know this, Narnie, which is why you need to believe me when I say that the wanker doesn't know half of the truth himself."

"Alex..."

"Just let me in," he pleaded. "Just for a minute, for his sake."

I opened the door a little wider, though not without vigilance. "Fine. For his sake."

"Yes, Narnie, for his sake."

Without another word and yet a thousand reservations, I motioned for him to enter. The usual ten steps to the living room seemed eternal. I saw a note Nana had left in the table saying she was off to Trader Joe's for burrito ingredients. Out with Maya. Twenty minutes tops, dear. Xoxo.

The sound of Alex dropping an envelope on our tea table in a rough, unsettling cacophony drew me back to the room. "I'm sure Ezra told you about Clara?"

I nodded slowly. "His sister, right? His dead sister?"

A moment of recognizance crossed his face. It was as if that was what he had believed too, but was suddenly on a mission to prove all of us wrong. "Open it. Go on."

I picked up the large yellow envelope. Shipped three days ago from San City in priority shipping, with stacks of paper tucked inside. I picked up the first of the many.

Al, it read in a distinctively cursive handwriting.

I am writing to you with a heavy and uncertain heart, hoping that you haven't forgotten me after my alleged death. I wouldn't blame you if you have because...well...you deserve to move on. As far as anyone is concerned, I am as good as dead, but I need you to understand that that man did not kill me that night. He threatened to do something worse...I will leave the details to your imagination in hopes that understanding me will come easier to you then.

Sienna decided to tag along with me. Sol's baby-by-eleven-minutes sister—you remember her, right? Sol, that sweet, understanding girl that Micah wrote a hundred songs about. Sienna was there that night with me when it happened and we're here together gathering evidence for our justice.

I am writing to you with a cause. I am horrible, I know, and I'm sorry. I wish everything was better for us and that I could tell you everything—but I signed a dumb NDA because the lawyers didn't want us spreading risk.

I'm worried sick about Ezra. I heard he's run away from Uncle Edem's. He'll be in Mama's caravan, maybe in the woods, under that tree we'd go to to smoke a joint. Keep an eye on him, alright? I love him so fucking much. God, he must be in pieces. Just keep him on track...make sure he doesn't break too many hearts because he's emotional. He's a big boy.

All of this is temporary. I'll be coming home soon. I love you.

With love,

Clara

I looked up from the letter to find Alex's anticipating gaze. "Clara is...alive?"

He nodded. The envelope carried all of Clara's letters, dating from the one I had just read, postmarked in August, to today. After all this time□—after all this grief□—she was alive? And Ezra could wake up one morning breathing the same air as his sister? Maybe the universe was not so cruel after all.

"Check the one I've bookmarked, Narns," Alex said. I suddenly saw in his conviction that his heart may have been with Larisa, but his soul was elsewhere, with Clara. "You know, the one with the blue ribbon."

I shakily rummaged through the stack to find that very one, my trembling hands barely holding the papers together as I read its words. Al, it began again.

The lawyers are there looking for evidence. A kind group of three. And I think I'm ready. Attached is some cash for tickets to San City. I've sent a scan of Ezra's passport. I'll be there to see him at the terminal. Please make sure he gets on the 4:30 PM plane on New Year's Day. It's crucial. And don't tell him. A morbid move, but I want to be the one to deliver the news to him that I'm alive. I hope you're okay. I've sent extra cash in case you decide to tag along.

Love,

Clara

"New Year's Day?" I repeated incredulously. "Are you fucking kidding me? That's today." I felt my eyes scan the clock by our living room door, which read half past nine. "There's less than seven hours before that flight. Mama would never let me."

"You don't have to go with him. Just convince him to go. That's all Lara wants."

"Convince him to go to San City on his own? How the hell am I supposed to do that?"

"Go with him then—I don't know. I'm just as confused as you are, Narnie."

I softened. "Why does he need to leave now though, Alex? Now, out of all times."

"The letters are all that I know."

"And the lawyers? Who are they?"

"No clue."

"Clara didn't tell you?"

He turned his gaze away from mine. "No."

A moment of silence settled between us. The ticking clock ebbed in its solitary rhythm, our only source of noise aside from the wind howling out on the avenue. I guess I had to do this. If I truly loved him, I had to find a way to get him to San City.

I looked to the side to find Alex's eyes peering into mine again. The tentative air loosened as I nodded, piecing the letters back together in the envelope. "I'll try."

He sighed in relief. "Thank you."

We were quiet again, the kind of quiet where we both knew it was time for Alex to leave, but neither of us wanted to part ways—not yet.

"You know," I finally said. "If you really care about him, why do you try so hard to make it seem like you don't?"

The corners of his lips trembled into a smile, as if the question had caught him off guard. "Because that is how we are, Narns. We have history. And history's always cursed. It never comes without misunderstandings, does it?"

"I guess not."

"He needed someone at the end of all this; I knew it wasn't me. But then I met you—and I knew from that day at the race that you were different. You were passionate, calm. He couldn't take his eyes off you that night. I knew then that the Larisa thing was history."

"You mean that?"

"Of course."

"I'll talk to him," I said again. He seemed to need more consolation.

He scratched the back of his neck. "I guess that's my cue to get the hell out of here."

"And mine too. I have someone I need to speak to, if we're going to San City tonight."

"Ezra?"

I shook my head. I had someone else in mind—Micah Henry, to be exact. I found him in his hospital room, absentmindedly fiddling a pen while gazing into nothingness. He arched an eyebrow upon seeing me.

"You lied to me, didn't you, Micah?" I said angrily. I held up the envelope Alex had left behind. "You know what's in here? Letters. Sealed, signed and delivered from San City."

He froze, realization seeping in. "What do you know?"

"I know that Clara Parker is alive."

"So she is."

"And you came back for her," I added. "You did, didn't you? But you also conveniently omitted the fact that you're not seeking justice for a dead person, Micah!"

"Lower your voice, Narnie."

"I will lower nothing."

"I knew that Clara was alive, but I also came back for myself—for my family."

"Fuck you, Micah."

"I'm telling the truth," he pressed. "Listen to me."

"How did all of this begin anyway? How did you get so involved?"

"It started in May..."

There was a certain urgency to Micah's breathing in Woodhaven hospital that evening. Strapped to the bed of the emergency room, his exhaustion betrayed him. Dark, prominent circles outlined his eyes fecklessly, as if on the brink of collapse.

The only thing separating him from the white waiting room was a sturdy glass wall. The row of seats left for his visitors were empty. Who could visit him, anyway? Nobody knew he was here.

He thought about his parents, about the devastation they would feel when they discovered the truth, and about Bella, his beautiful and pretentious little sister—and then the dark haired beauty, the invader of his guilty thoughts despite his vehement efforts to forget her. He envisioned the lackluster look on their faces, ridden with despair as they came to terms with the fact that Micah Henry was going to die.

He could not tell them—would not. He was selfish, he supposed. He wanted the pleasure of seeing them happy until the very end. For his own sake, he would keep this a secret.

His chest constricted in his ribcage, his beating heart palpable against his bones as he stared directly ahead. The insipid white of the hospital walls peered back at him, ensnaring him in the ways of loneliness too much for any one human to bear.

The doctor came in eventually, a clipboard on his hand. His gaze revealed the news his lips struggled to say. "The results, Micah," he began rather diffidently. "They're not optimistic."

"How much longer?" Micah asked.

"A year. Maybe half a year more, at most."

He nodded, ingesting the information even though it numbed him. But upon closing his eyes, he imagined the delicate olive of Sol's face and the way her hands would wrap around his neck in consolation. That was all it took for a little life to be restored within him.

When Micah was discharged from the hospital later that evening, he purchased an overdue flight back to suburbia. His best friend, Ciara, helped him home. He was going to withdraw his enrollment from university the very next day and submit his letter of resignation to his boss before leaving for good. He planned it all on the cab on the way to his apartment.

And so the next day, he arrived at his office not without a re-solve. He briefly reconsidered his decision. After all, he had spent his entire life working towards this dream. Over those days when his parents had shamed him for not becoming a doctor, when they had told him that the Ivy League was a faraway pipe dream for him because they were not wealthy, he had nevertheless persisted.

Success was a lonely road to follow when you had bigger dreams for yourself than your family did for you. And it would perhaps be reasonable to resign from his dreams if he was met with consistent failure, but Micah was a precocious young man. At the age of twenty, he had already been recruited by his dream firm.

He stepped in through the glass frames eventually, plastering a blithe expression on his face. "Morning Phoebe," he greeted the receptionist at the front desk, loosening his grasp on the cup of Starbucks on his hand.

Tucking a strand of her blonde hair behind her ear, she looked up. "Oh, Micah? Didn't expect to see you today!"

He laughed, spinning in the direction of the elevator. "Just some unfinished business to take care of. I'll see you."

"Of course," she replied, with a laugh only he could bring about. "Bye Micah."

He loosened his tie, unfastening the topmost button of his shirt as he pressed the button to the eighteenth floor. There were a lot of things he'd expected to see transpiring in that firm that evening, but who he saw standing by the counter made his eyes narrow in disbelief. He tentatively took several steps closer, his suspicions proven when a familiar pair of almond eyes met his. "Clara?"

"Micah," she breathed out.

"You know some coincidences that are so strange that they make you reconsider everything? That was one of them. And Clara hadn't come there looking for me. She was there because she was told that Larson, Amin and Associates, the firm I worked for, was the best in the country for cases of her father's kind."

A rush of curiosity overrode my body. "She left Holden for her father?"

"Confidential information, Narns."

"But why did she fake her death? Why didn't she tell Ezra?"

"I can't say."

"And you were able to pick up her case even though you're not a barred attorney?"

"This past summer, I was working under one of the partners. Your mother, Narnie. She saw that the case was in Holden and picked it up immediately. I couldn't quit then, not after seeing her."

"Larson, Amin and Associates," I said, realization seeping in. "Of course."

He stood there silently, his body calm despite the burden of information.

"So Clara's safe, right?" I asked. I held up the letters on my hand. "Alex gave me these. Wants me to take Ezra to San City on her word."

"She had mentioned that."

"So we should go?"

"You should do whatever your heart tells you to do."

"Great advice coming from the man who just loves listening to his heart."

He chuckled briefly, the gesture not quite meeting his eyes.

"How are you otherwise, Micah?" I digressed. "The sickness. Is it spreading?"

"I'm out on paid leave, love. I'm chilling. And I'm on a new set of treatments."

"Have you told anyone?"

"Sol," he said, taking me by surprise. "She visited the other day."

"And did you tell her you love her?"

"No."

"Will you ever?"

"She hates me. I broke her heart."

"But you have a reason."

He chuckled humorlessly.

"Who's working on Clara's case then? Is it just Mama?"

"Don't worry about that. You take your boy to San City. Give him that little surprise."

"But—"

"And have fun there. You both need a little break."

I knew then that it would be cruel to keep him here. That was all the assurance I needed to continue planning our escape. I took out the cash from the envelope and gave Micah the letters before leaving for the pizzaria. As I left through the sliding doors, I was met with a frosty suburban morning. The pavements were armored in snow, the branches of the trees cast in a blinding porcelain. And along with it the wind danced, brushing the snow off our cobbled roofs and gazebos.

The journey to the pizzeria was brief. I saw the familiar neon sign eventually. The bulbs in the L no longer functional, it read Car Pizzeria, flickering every now and then. I parked in the lot as the sun declared her secession from the clouds, brightening the vicinity. The icy Holden air rekindled in me a longing for the long gone summer heat.

I walked around to the front of the shop, stopping when I saw Ezra's back on the other side of the glass wall that barricaded his counter from the main street. He wasn't alone. I saw in the glass my crumbling body reflected as my eyes fell upon Larisa's face merely centimeters away from his. Her fingers were trailing across his chest in a gesture of intimacy. I whisked in without thinking.

"Tell me you feel something," she began breathlessly, letting her fingers linger. "When I touch you there, Ezra." She let herself explore the labyrinth that was his body, her ambitious eyes disclosing not even a trickle of her ignominy as her fingertips trailed to his shoulders. Her eyes penetrated his before landing on mine. "And there."

I prepared my heart for its collapse, but it never did, because Ezra then grabbed the hands of the only woman he had ever claimed to love; interlacing his fingers around her wrist like shoelaces, he brought the face of her hands to his lips for a kiss. "I feel nothing," he said, letting it drop.

I stood on the linoleum floor as every doubt I had vaporized into nothingness. That one action would assure me for eternity that if anything in this world deserved to exist, it was a chance for Ezra and I.

Her face cast with embarrassment, she shoved past him. Her shoulders brushed mine on her journey out the door. When the bell jingled, signaling her departure, when he then turned around, our paths crossed intensely, his candid eyes finding mine with an unearthly serenity, a little like a forager coming home after a meaningful journey in the wilderness, only to realize that what he sought was in front of him all along. There was so much appreciation in that one glance that I wanted nothing more than to drown in him, in his one glance.

I fumbled for words. "What about now, Ezra? What do you feel?"

His lips twitched into the smile that had somehow become my sanctuary. "Everything," he murmured, filling the spaces between us with the warmth of his presence.

I looked up at his face, centimeters away. "And your pretty eyed lady?"

He chuckled as he kissed my forehead. "Didn't we talk about this?"

"We did, but—"

"She was just a pretty eyed lady, Narnie. Somewhere along the way of waiting, I found someone better, a lady with a pretty soul."

My hands fell limply to their sides. I walked over to the counter and took a seat on one of the stools, saying nothing as he brewed us tea.

"A morning treat," he said, sliding me a cup.

My fingers trembled as I reached for it. And of course, he read me without a word.

"You okay?"

Just say it, Narnie. Lexington University. Open house. It's tomorrow. In San City. But what if he says no? Even if I wanted to go, there was no guarantee he would come with me.

He placed his hands on the counter, forcing me to look at him. "What's wrong?"

"I—I wanted to show you something," I stammered. "That's why I came."

"We'll go and see it after seven, okay? When I get off."

"No, Ezra."

He arched an eyebrow. "No?"

"It—it's in San City."

"Then we'll go to San City."

"Can we go tonight?"

He raised an eyebrow. "Tonight?"

"There's a flight at four and I just—"

He leveled his head with mine, his lips morphing into a smile. "You think I would ever turn down an adventure with you?" He planted a kiss on my nose. "We'll go."

I thanked the universe for conspiring in my favor. I arrived back home to find Nana in the living room, knitting a scarf. "Happy new year, Nana," I said, enveloping her in a hug.

She looked up, laughing a little. "You too, dear."

"Any plans tonight?"

"The Henrys have invited us for dinner, if that's okay with you?"

"Actually," I began shyly. I slipped next to her on the sofa. "I was wondering..."

She looked up, unfazed. "Nothing you request can shock me anymore, Narnie."

"I need to get on a flight to San City—tonight."

She dropped her crochet on her lap. "Yet you constantly take me by surprise."

I slid closer to her and told her everything. I started from the very beginning with Ezra to what we found to be suspect about his father's conviction. I told her about the past few months, omitting only our suspicion about Edem, and about how Alex had stopped by this morning to deliver the news that Clara Parker was still alive. "It would be cruel, Nana, to let this chance slip by."

How could she say no to that? And I knew, deep in her heart, that she knew Holden was unsafe for the time being, at least until Mama proved the truth about the killer.

I remember a sigh that lasted a little too long, a face inevitably strung with concern and slowly, Nana's relenting face. "You'll call me," she demanded. "Three times a day. Morning, noon and night."

"Of course, Nana."

"And you'll be back before school is in session?"

I nodded. "A few days tops."

"Your mother is going to kill me."

And just like that, I had her okay. She drove me to the airport that night. The car ride seemed to stretch on for eternity—and I would've believed it had, had the clock on the dashboard not reassured me that only minutes had gone by. When we arrived, the lanes by the departure were so packed that Nana kissed my cheek and asked me if I could take it from there. I nodded and left.

I saw him just as I exited the car. He was waiting under the sign that read Terminal Six, a duffle bag slung over his shoulders. His eyes were on his phone.

I sucked in my cheeks to resist a smile that was so excruciatingly inappropriate at a time like this. He was just—just...sigh. A simple glance rekindled the same flame; and I wondered if the human body could gather enough heat to set itself on fire. For now I may have been at equilibrium: a flowing river, a crisp midwinter's night and a rainy Saturday, until I no longer was. I could never fathom the person I became around him.

"Hello, hello!" I said, rushing toward him.

He lifted his head from his phone, a small smile creeping onto his face.

"I hope I didn't make you wait too long."

"Not at all," he said, brushing himself off the wall. "Ready?"

I nodded.

We boarded the 4:30 flight to San City. I fell asleep on his shoulder only to wake up as we landed.

"Narnie," I heard him murmur, his breath fanning my face.

I stirred.

"Baby, wake up," he continued.

I gumbled, patting him away.

"Narnie," he repeated a little louder. "Wake up!"

My eyes flung open. "What?"

"We're here."

I yawned, lifting my head. "Here?"

"Your city," he told me with a smile. "I thought it never slept."

I mustered a smile of my own, however weak. "Right."

We left the plane then. As we walked through the exit lanes and found ourselves at the terminal, my heartstrings fluttered incessantly. Clara was somewhere within this crowd of peering, anticipating eyes, waiting for Ezra. It was far too obvious when he saw her because his fingertips desperately found mine. His eyes had widened, his lips parting in awe and his face pale. "No," he conjured in disbelief.

I followed his eyes and knew. After all, she had his eyes, the same light green, dotted with an identical verdance. The smile on her ashen face extended to her cheeks as her irises danced with mirth at the sight of her brother before her.

"Welcome home, Ezra," I murmured, giving his hand a tight squeeze and leading the way.

CHAPTER 14

There was stillness. For a fleeting moment, it was as if there was no time. "Clara," Ezra murmured. It may have been a hum.

Tears pooled down Clara's porcelain cheeks, her cries interrupted only by fragments of her own laughter. She held onto him with every fiber of her being, fear incarcerating her eyes at the thought of letting go. It was as if she thought he would disappear if she did.

Underneath it all, Ezra's soft fingertips trailed across my thumb: his unspoken gratitude.

"Ezra," she whispered over and over again. A soft succession of hums.

"Narnie," he murmured later that night. The city lay below us, its movements a silhouette under Clara's dilapidating fire escape. The illuminating red of headlights glowed on the damp pavements that cried hope and despair. As the honking of the vehicles disrupted his raspy breaths, I saw in his eyes the reflection of the cityscape I had cherished for all of these months—and those very same eyes, once lamenting the past, now held a promise of the future. He pulled me into kisses that lingered for a little longer than they should have, his gestures stifled only by his sobbing. "How could you do it, Narnie? How could you keep everything from me?"

I was the least bit interested in his words. I was far away, somewhere in cloud nine, coming to terms with the fact that I had fallen incoherently and quite foolishly in love with Ezra Parker. With every passing moment, I was plunging further into a cliff with no end in sight. I was falling in love with him, hoping that his affection would shield me as I collided with the ground, but no one gets by with just a minor scrape after falling from such great heights. I was bound to a catastrophe.

"Come in for dinner, you two," Clara said, opening her window for us.

"I'm sorry, Ezra," I began, but he looked directly ahead, plastering his eyes on the silhouette of a moving man.

"It's like the universe is giving me a second chance."

"Maybe it is."

"I hope so. I really hope so."

"Ezra, Narnie—dinner!" Clara called out again.

We slipped back in through the windows. As I washed my hands and helped Clara set the table, Ezra disappeared behind us to freshen up. A clandestine smile gracing her face, a face that looked more and more like Ezra with each passing moment, she handed me a stack of plates for the dining table. "You know, Narnie, I thought I was losing my mind when I saw Ezra coming out of that terminal with a girl. I wondered for a moment if I was hallucinating—if it was really him."

"I'm actually Alex," I said in the most Alex voice I could conjure. I placed the plates on the table and met her eyes. "I've been meaning to tell you, Clara...I got a sex change."

She burst out in laughter, removing her spinach pies from the oven. "God, please no. You're too beautiful to be that dirtbag."

"I guess hatred for Alex runs in the family."

"Oh, I don't hate him. I love him. But that's our problem, isn't it? We always end up falling for the dirtbags."

"All of us except me," I said softly.

"Maybe you are the only exception," Clara said with another laugh.

"Exception to what?" Ezra said, walking into the room.

Clara placed our individual spanakopitas on our plates. "We were just about to discuss if you're a dirtbag, before you so rudely interrupted, little brother."

He sat down on the chair closest to me, pouting. "Am I?"

"Of course you're not," I said. I squeezed his nose before helping Clara gather the dirty oven trays in the sink.

"Sit down and start, love," she said, motioning towards the table. "Ezra, can you grab the tzatziki? It's in the fridge."

I sat down and waited for Clara to finish. I thought about the family dinners we would have: Nana, Clara, Ezra, Mama and I. Maybe he could help Mama wrap momos—her favorite Nepali dumplings. Maybe we could sit down with virgin mimosas and toast to this beautiful, cruel world and the happiness we had found within it.

"How is it, Narnie?" Clara asked, breaking me out of my reverie. She took a seat beside Ezra.

"You are officially my favorite cook," I said, taking my first bite. "It's delicious."

Ezra scrunched his nose. "Stop lying to her, Narnie."

Clara silently motioned towards him, mouthing Dirtbag to me.

He chuckled, his cheeks turning red. "I'm only joking. You know it's delicious, Lar."

"It's Mom's recipe," she explained. She ruffled his hair. "He can tell you."

He smiled warily, saying nothing.

Clara dug into her own plate, looking up at us. "Did you two meet in Holden?"

"Yeah," Ezra said. He started from the beginning, from the days when I was nothing more than a passing thought to those that felt banal without our adventures across suburbia. "I was smug about her, Lar. I didn't think that I would like her so much, you know?"

"I don't know about that...He was pretty crazy about me from the beginning."

Clara smiled at the two of us. "Have you introduced her to Uncle Edem, Ez?"

A premonitory silence materialized at the mention of Edem. Ezra's uneasiness manifested through his chewing, slow and contained, as he swallowed, shaking his head.

"How is he—Uncle Edem?"

The silence, thick and heavy, was broken only by the sound of Ezra's utensil meeting his plate. "I wouldn't know, Clara."

She furrowed her eyebrows. "Did something happen?"

Ezra hesitated. "After what happened to Mama—to you—we thought that maybe he may have been responsible."

She looked at him as if the notion was so bizarre that she was astonished we had entertained it at all. And then she laughed, an amazed, dumbfounded laugh, taking us both by surprise. "Don't tell me you thought Uncle Edem murdered Mom, Ezra," she said. When Ezra merely sat there, saying nothing, she raised her fingers to her temples. "God damn it, Ezra, you innocent little boy. Uncle Edem is one of the people trying to help us uncover who did it. What in the world would lead you to think it was him?"

Maybe it was desperation. Maybe it was his urgent longing for an answer. Maybe it was because he needed an indication—any indication—that it wasn't his father that had done it, that he hadn't, on the brim of passion or irrationality, taken the life of a woman he had so intimately loved.

"I don't know," he relented. "I just—I don't know."

"And you Narnie? You believed this?"

I looked away from her, my cheeks shrouding with warmth.

"Jesus, you two. This is why we don't put two eighteen year olds in charge of a murder case. Have you spoken to Uncle Edem at all?"

Ezra looked down at his spanakopita, only halfway eaten, now cold. "No."

Clara released a sigh. "I thought Uncle Edem was taking care of you. He told me you had moved into Mama's caravan, but he never told me you had shunned him away. Did you know this, Narnie?"

"I—"

"She found a bottle of benzodiazepine in his car, Lara. Tell me it isn't odd that he had the only drug they had found in Mom's system when she died. And don't you dare say he has insomnia. You and I both know very well that he doesn't."

"Did you ever consider that there was another reason for it—that maybe Uncle Edem had an explanation?"

"Lara—"

"No, no Lara. You're being irrational, Ezra."

"But the benzodiazepine," he said, his voice barely a whisper.

"That's from the night he found me. The night that changed everything."

"The night Mom died?"

"The night Jestem Matar got to me and Sienna Flores."

"Jestem Matar? Who is Jestem Matar?"

If you looked at her, which many people did, the first thing you noticed was the birthmark above her lip, just like her sister's. Physically, they may have been indistinguishable, Sol and Sienna, but Sienna's stubbornness had led her to impulsively dye her dark hair an atypical white. This was at the age of twelve to avoid dull comparisons to her sister. The eccentric color was rejected by their strict mother, but Sienna was adamant—and so it became a symbol of her identity as she grew older, the only thing differentiating her from her precocious younger sister.

That may have been the first thing that drew Jestem Matar to her, the delectable milkiness of her hair, a glimpse into her distant, stubborn personality. He would tell her one evening that Clara Parker was never in the plan; it had only ever been her.

"Jestem Matar, just twenty five then, seduced poor Sienna over glasses of wine in upscale restaurants in Fort Montgomery. And what seventeen year old girl doesn't dream of her knight in a shining armor, sweeping her away like that? Mature and predatory, with wine clearer than his intentions. And that's the most haunting part. That night, we had gone to Pensavo, an Italian place on the edge of Lowell and Myrtle. He was Sienna's exciting old man. He was charming—really charming. And we ended up taking a late night cab back to his apartment without knowing fully what we were getting ourselves into. Did we think we would wake up the next morning, completely disoriented with no recollection of the previous night? No one thinks that. No one."

When Clara awoke the next morning, she was a lone ranger in that battlefield, tied to a bed as if in a nightmarish process of being exorcised. Her body writhing in the pain of the unknown, she scanned her surroundings to uncover the most beautiful room she had ever seen: indigo walls garnished with Renaissance era frames, vintage and gilded, with landscapes of mountains and the like. On one end of the room lay a bookcase built from the remnants of demolished oakwood, carrying an exquisite collection of ancient novels and on its opposing end: a long cabinet and the bed atop which she lay. As her eyes descended to the floor, she saw the violet satin of her dress.

She winced at the sight of her naked body before her, shouting the only words she could conjure: a weak, unconvincing "Help!" but only silence followed, her lips producing no more than a series of incoherent, inaudible noises—and all at once, she thought about Sienna, about how they had both left Pensavo draped in Jestem's arms. Now, Sienna was nowhere to be seen.

Clara's only companion was a religious caricature on the bookshelf, its head bobbing back and forth. She looked at it, at its large eyes and stoic lips. Its sinister face morphed into Jestem's despite their bearing no resemblance, the dim sunlight streaming in through the scarlet drapes camouflaging his uncannily bloodshot eyes.

Clara's eyes wandered to his bare chest, failing to reconcile with his naked body, void of dignity and shame, and when his callous fingertips caressed her thighs, she lay her eyes on the divine caricature, silently begging it for mercy. A solitary tear descended down her cheeks as Jestem entered her, but salvation never came.

"That was the moment I lost my faith in God," she said while Ezra sat on the chair, his sobs punctuating her every word: the desolate reaction of a man who too was void of all faith. Clara swallowed, her breathing shallow and labored, shame tainting her voice despite her knowledge that Jestem's transgressions were not her to own. "I saw it that morning, Ezra, the pills on his nightstand—and I knew. I knew he had been the one to kill Momma."

She looked into her brother's eyes for his reaction, her lips quivering at his fading warmth, now reduced to vacancy, and in her helplessness she turned toward me. I slid behind his trembling body and held him, letting his movements undulate every inch of my bones. "It's okay, baby," I whispered, resting my chin on his head. "Lara's okay. Look. She's right here and she loves you so much. She's okay."

He placed his hands on his lap. I reached to squeeze them but Clara beat me to it, her fingers finding his—her silent assurance.

"I never wanted to leave you, Ez," she said quietly. "I left because Jestem tried to kill me—and he thought he succeeded. And I couldn't bear the thought of living in that town with the knowledge that my rapist was still on the loose, my rapist who in all likelihood murdered my mother and framed my father and tried to do the same to me? I needed to come here without the burden of being followed. I needed to come for Dad."

Ezra finally parted his lips to speak, taking us by surprise. "Have you spoken to him at all—Dad?"

She nodded glumly.

"And Uncle Edem? Does he know?"

She nodded again, the gesture hollow. "I woke up in the woods, buried alive, with nothing but a bottle of those pills. His twisted idea of mockery, I suppose. I took it to Uncle Edem when I got out of there. And maybe Narnie found it because it never left his car. I swore him to secrecy that he wouldn't tell anyone—not until Dad was out. I couldn't have him tell you because you had your own life, and I couldn't take on the responsibility of bringing you with me. Not then."

"Why call me here now?"

"We have an entire team down in Holden, working on Dad's case. And with the disappearances becoming more frequent and the consistency of the benzodiazepine, the new evidence for an appeal is already there. They finally set a court date, Ez."

He took in the information, saying nothing and offering very little emotion.

"Ezra," Clara said, releasing an exasperated sigh. She pulled his hands to her chest, smothering them in an overdue embrace. "Are you listening to me at all? The court date is set. For this week. After which Dad's going to be free, little one. You know what that means, don't you? We're almost at the end. We're finally going to be a family again."

CHAPTER 15

I thought about Papa that night. Tucked under covers with Ezra Parker on his sister's sofa, I thought about him while Ezra and I breezed through horror movies. It was halfway into our second movie that the nostalgia became too much to bear.

I excused myself and slid out of Clara's apartment—and I saw in the damp January streets the daylight of late August, of our street, Madison Avenue, after a vicious downpour, when all the neighborhood kids gathered to float paper sailboats on the puddles forming on the sides of the roads. In the memory, I am ten and Papa is watching me from the steps of our townhouse, his tender glances warming our cul-de-sac.

"Are they your best friends, Narnie?" he would ask me, referring to my friends, Trevor and Lilian. "Are you going to grow old with them?"

"No, Papa," I wanted to say to him. "But Micah, Ezra, Sol, Anderson, Teo and Bella—with them I will."

"How do you know, my sweet?"

"I just do."

I turned the corner, debilitated by the longing to hear him say, one last time, "Narnie, my baby girl. I am so proud of you."

I wondered what would happen if Papa, like Clara, had faked his death. What if he was still out there, wandering this beautiful, cruel world, running away from something bigger than himself? Was his death just our collective hallucination? But how could any of it be, when I had seen his body taken away in an ivory casket just months ago—when it had been taken to Woodhaven cemetery for only the earthworms to break into?

I boarded a crosstown bus to Woodhaven cemetery, wondering what I was looking for on my way there. Maybe it was closure, to wake up one day no longer affected by his death. Maybe it was something else entirely.

The hours veered toward midnight, revealing the disparate alcoves of San City: its carefree adolescents, the sons and daughters of the wealthy socialites, its low wage workers, toiling to make ends meet, and its university students, their lives intersecting on the late night busses and metros despite their worlds being far apart, the latter of them intoxicated and in the process of forgetting. I tried to imagine that Micah was one of them, that he was on this bus on New Year's Day, going home with the people he loved most.

The graveyard was the same as I remembered it, surrounded by rows of weathering granite, bare willow trees and a shallow pond of stillwater. I followed the only path to Papa's tombstone. It was covered in season old ivy, with a case of white roses resting underneath the granite engraving: Here lies Theodore, a father, a husband and a beloved son. I kneeled before the roses, picking one up. Someone had been here—but who?

"I was wondering if I would find you here tonight, Narnie."

My blood went cold—and when I turned around, there she was: my mother, Maya Larson, who's months of neglect had convinced me that she was as good as dead.

"Taking a flight to San City on New Year's Day with a boy you met no less than five months ago. A bit careless, don't you think?"

I opened my mouth to speak, but every word I knew suddenly left my mind. I wanted to ask her what right she had to look for me. She hadn't even shown her face on New Year's day.

Mama took the rose from my hand and released a sigh, spreading its petals on the body of his grave. "I miss him too, you know. I miss him everyday. I miss him so much that my bones ache at the simple thought of him, like they're missing a part, like my limbs were torn out and I'm being tested to live on without them." And for the first time, her stoic countenance gave themselves away to the reality of her grief.

There she lay, Maya Larson, a mother, a wife and a victim of her cruel destiny—but maybe we were all a victim of our cruel destinies. Maybe that was something we consented to by the fact of our being alive.

"I miss him, Mama," I said. "I miss him so much."

She looked at me wistfully with eyes that could cry no more. "Come here," she whispered. When I just stood there, saying nothing, she ushered me closer. "Come."

I carried my body toward her, listless and heavy, until she enveloped me in the familiar spearmint of her embrace. Maybe we were there for a minute—maybe more. We were there until her gentle sobs subsided into a quieter night, leaving us with nothing but the hollowed out memory of what once was. Maybe remembering was the root of all suffering and all of life was a journey to forget, until our eventual death, when our memories became no more.

"I'd bring him back for you if I could, you know," I told her. "Even if it meant I had to take his place."

"And I would never let you do that, my dear, not in a million years."

"But—"

"No buts. Do you know how happy we were the day you came into our lives? Seven pounds and always smiling, I was convinced your father would never look at another woman again. And how disappointed he would be, if he knew what has happened to us. Forgive me, baby. Forgive me."

I held her closely to give her a body to hold, convinced that the forgiveness she was seeking was not mine, but somebody else's. And above us, the stars flickered in delight, teasing us with the possibility that Papa had heard us—that he had forgiven her. But how could he? He was dead.

We took an Uber back home to Madison Avenue. It was the same as we had left it, a little like walking into a repeating dream, an old comfort, a tucked away memory. We took our coats off and sat in the living room, talking about everything until I had spilled over almost every detail of my life about Ezra.

"They're good people, the Parkers," Mama said. "They're a lot to take on, but they're good people."

"He needs me now, Mama."

"Be safe, my sweet Narnie."

"I am safe. We have Clara."

"That you do—but does Clara offer protection against eighteen year old boys?"

"Mama, I—"

"Just joking, my dear. No need to take it so seriously."

It was nearly sunrise by the time I returned to Clara's bedroom, but I found Ezra wide awake, staring at his ceiling. He tilted his head at the noise of my retreating footsteps. "Went off on an adventure?"

I slipped my coat off my body and slid next to him. "Something like that."

He snaked his arms around me, leaving an airy kiss on my shoulder. "It's good to have you back."

I closed my eyes and exploited his warmth, counting sheep until I fell asleep. It was good to be back.

CHAPTER 16

We felt the calm before the storm. The calm was so beautiful that I wondered if I had stepped into a dream. It was a dream, those late winter days, as Ezra and I explored San City, spending most of our hours by the harbor where I had my first kiss, where Lilian, Trevor and I would often go to waste time. We passed the time reading poetry and getting high—and when the day faded into yet another night, I took him home to Mama, where they bonded over the foreign words of Spinoza's Ethics. "That boy's a spitting image of your father, Narnie," she would say. "Full of so much life and passion, I can tell he's going to go far."

The three of us were in Mama's kitchen that night, following a recipe for Chicken Biryani, when I got a call from Isabella. Her frantic voice filling the receiver's end, her sobs drowned out Mama's laughter in the background. I excused myself from the kitchen, waiting for her to deliver the news that Micah was dead.

"The serial killer tried to attack Sol," she said instead, taking me by surprise.

Sol was in a gas station when it happened, scouring its mini mart for an ice cream sandwich. Dawn crevassed the Port Orion skies, the waves of the Hudson lapping against the dilapidated lumber of a nearby boardwalk. It was early enough that the morning cardinals had invaded every telephone line in sight, their cries severing the passersby from their nightly slumber. Under the gentle glimmer of tangerine breaking through the clouds, she picked up a sandwich manufactured by Daddy's Dairy and slid it into her coat pocket. Then she went by the boardwalk, as she did every morning, for her daily dose of serenity.

She had taken up the routine after Micah's departure. Every morning, she would sit by the boardwalk and watch the sun rise. It provided a temporary release from the prison that was her racing mind, providing a temporary solace in this otherwise cruel world.

"She was sitting there, minding her own business, when a man masquerading as a police officer approached her and said something about the boardwalk being off limits until seven. Somehow convinced her to get in his car so he could drive her home. She's so shaken, Narnie. She hasn't said a word."

"Where is she now?"

"Micah just brought her back here from the sheriffs and told us what happened. There are reporters swarming our house. It's insane."

"Micah? Was he there too?"

"Yeah..."

He had gone to drop off a few documents when she arrived, the hem of her jacket torn beneath her trembling hands. Four pairs of unsuspecting eyes met her breathless figure, all of them equally surprised. The first person she recognized was Micah, standing behind the counter with Mr. Adams, an officer on duty. Micah raised his head, his eyes finding Sol's.

"I need to use the bathroom," she said, her voice shaky against her lips.

"Go," the officer said.

Sol placed her fingers over the hem of her coat to conceal its unwinding threads. Avoiding Micah's eyes, she ran into the bathroom, oblivious to the footsteps trailing behind her as she sunk to the floor, the coarse wall piercing the skin under her jacket. Buying her face in her arms, she cried into her knees until her tragedies came undone.

It was a few minutes later that warm, stout arms snaked around her waist. She didn't need to look up to know the owner of those arms—those firm, knowing arms that shyly hindered on her hips, soft fingers resting comfortingly, pulling her closer into a safe haven that smelled more and more like coffee.

She raised her head, burying it in his shoulder. An unspoken, mutual understanding passed between the two of them. As they sat there elapsed in time, she cried freely into Micah's arms for everything that happened and even more for all that had been lost.

They must have been at it for hours. They stayed until the illuminating glow of evening subsided into the wistful darkness of dusk, leaving them in the narrow vicinity with nothing to guide them but Sol's erratic sobs. Micah wondered what he should have been doing, if it was okay for him to hold her and if she had cried for him, just like this, all those months ago.

"I—I need a minute," she finally sputtered, her voice lacking the conviction that accompanied most of her words. "I need to clean up, Micah."

He looked at her, at the mascara trickling down her eyes, and her pink, plump lips, coated in their saliva. He wanted nothing more than to hold her until his very last breath. "I can help."

"Yeah?"

"Uh, yeah," he said, her question for some reason taking him by surprise. He fumbled around for nothing in particular.

She swallowed as she looked at him. She had never seen him so helpless.

He stood up and turned on the faucet, letting the water run. Then he turned around, extending his hands for her to take. She released a mellow breath as their fingers intertwined. In the bleak vicinity within the station's walls, with the wintry air piercing their skin through the untended window, she shivered under his touch.

"Maybe you should go," she said at last.

He pretended that those words didn't hurt him. "Yeah?"

She nodded. So he did. He saw her again about an hour later, when he was out on the curb smoking a cigarette. He dropped it as he saw her emerge, stepping over its dimly lit bud in an effort to hide it. But she raced to her car, avoiding him as if he were the plague. She was like this, he remembered, curt and temperamental.

His heart hastened as he approached her, his hands shaky and his cheeks burning. But the collected way in which he presented himself deceived her. As he reached her car, she looked at her intruder, at his soft eyes that did more than just glance—it was like they were devouring her, those irises of his.

Already inside, Sol unrolled her windows.

He leaned over, leveling his head with hers. "Avoiding me again, Solita?"

She cast her timid glance away from him, thinking about that day in the hospital when he had told her about his cancer—when he had then told her that it was best for her to stay away.

He leaned in to grab her wrist. He didn't know why he did that.

"Please," she exhaled, yanking it away. "Why are you even here, Micah?"

He wondered why he was there—why he had stuck around for this long after seeing her—but of course, the answer was clear. It always had been. It was because he was madly in love with her.

"Because," he said weakly.

"Because?"

"Because..."

"Because?"

"Because I want to know what happened. Why else?"

The fragment of hope that had overtaken her face evaporated into nothingness. "I've already spoken to the sheriff. And I don't want to speak to you—so you can leave."

"Are you mad at me, Solita?"

Her eyes widened. "Don't you dare, Micah," she said, her voice just above a whisper. "Don't you dare question my anger. If anything, I have the right to be angry."

He recoiled, regretting his tone. As she looked at him, she looked different then. She was less of the girl he knew when he did love her, her innocence no longer intact, but he knew that this woman before him, whoever she had become, he could love more—he already did. Of course he did.

I'm sorry, he wanted to say. He wanted to shower her with the affection she deserved—to kiss her until his senses numbed. If only she knew. Misery by silence.

They stayed there without a word, watching nothing but the desolate parking lot before them, the zooming of one or two cars passing on vacant occasions. No words exchanged, not a gesture enacted, Sol and Micah existed in the tender silence they knew best. Eventually, he released a sigh, reaching to caress her. She let his fingers linger.

"Come home with me?"

She took in a breath that made her entire body convulse.

"We can talk about it," he continued. "We'll go back to my place. We'll talk. Everything will be fine, I promise."

How can everything be fine, Micah? You're dying, she wanted to say. She settled for a curt "Fine."

"Fine?"

"Fine," she repeated. "Let's do it."

"Right here?" he jested, raising an eyebrow. When she shook her head in mild disapproval, he stood up, chuckling to himself. "Just joking, love. Ready to go?"

She nodded. She led the way with her car. The roads were astonishingly clear for Holden, the darkness only deepening as they parked their cars on his driveway.

His room was the same as she remembered it: tidy and organized, perhaps excruciatingly so. She caught a glimpse of a photo of her, Bella and Micah on his nightstand. It was a long time ago—it must have been—but as she closed her eyes to recall the memory, she remembered it as if it was yesterday.

She went up to it before Micah could hide the photograph, stopping his fingers before they removed the only trace of her that he seemed to have left in here. "Freshman year," she said. "Daddy's Dairy, right?"

He nodded, recalling the whipped cream on Sol's nose, his fingertips trailing across her skin as he wiped off the white and the red that had coated her cheeks ever so shyly. The rush. The hopes. The possibility. Then the epiphanies. The realization that nothing in this world could be permanent, really.

"Daddy's dairy," he responded faintly.

"Bella looks so happy here."

"We all do."

She sat on the edge of his chair, toying with the button of her coat. "Do you ever wonder, Micah?"

"Wonder?"

"Wonder what would've happened to us if you had stayed with me that night—if you hadn't left?"

He kneeled before her, placing his hands on the clutches of his chair. He pulled the chair toward him, finding her cheeks damp with her tears. When had she begun to cry? "Micah," she whispered, collapsing onto him. He felt her weight all at once.

He held her by the back of her hair, pressing her into him. As he placed a hand on her waist, she curled deeper into his shoulder. "I—I just—I missed this. This smell. It smells like home."

He let her cry until her words ran dry—until he plucked up the courage to ask her what was wrong. Her eyes were hollow, the vacant eyes of a woman who he could have sworn felt nothing but disgust for him—but she came around eventually, her quivering arms reaching to unbutton her coat. "I'll show you," she said at last.

He watched her as she parted from him, the ghost of her touch lingering on his skin. She looked like a poltergeist, her face laced with love and disdain. Wiping her tears with the sleeve of her coat, she stood up, removing her clothes and dropping it onto the floor. His eyes widened in confusion as she lifted the ends of her velvet dress. An unmistakable sensation of nostalgia aroused his senses as his lint found its home in her velvet.

She peered down at him, her arms overridden with goosebumps and her body naked against the forlorn air. He saw fresh marks all over her body, palpable against her skin, a mix of purple and scarlet. She led his hands through each one.

Micah was a virtuous man, but then and there, he may have considered murder. "Who?"

"You know," she whispered, bringing a hand to his jaw. "This hurts, Micah. But nothing, not these bruises or the scratches, hurts as much as the day you left." She paused momentarily, looking away, and when she looked at him again, the intensity of her gaze devoured every bit of life left in him. "You didn't even say goodbye."

He was at a loss for words. If there was a moment to tell her the truth, it was then. "Forgive me," he murmured instead. It was weak, not the tone of a man who wanted to be forgiven.

"Never," she said, but she had already forgiven him. She had done it before he had asked.

He felt his protectiveness return. "Who did this to you?" he pressed. His murderous eyes betrayed him all too well, and for once, Sol considered the possibility that he still loved her.

"I—I don't know. I just—I reported him."

He took a deep breath.

"They said he matched the description of the serial killer."

"What did he do to you, Solita?"

"I don't want to talk about it anymore."

That's okay. I just want you to know that I love you, he wanted to say. He brought his hands to her bare waist, placing an innocuous kiss on the side of her thigh. When she shivered, he reached for the comforter lying on his bed and wrapped it around her body. And she began crying again, at his actions and lack thereof. "Did you ever want me, Micah?" she asked him. When he turned to meet her gaze, she had already looked away.

He sat on the floor beside her, his head spinning in circles. Tucking a desolate strand of her hair behind her ear, he let a moment of silence pass between them. "I want you more than I've ever wanted anybody, bub," he finally said. "But not here—not like this."

She eased into his comforter.

He scooped her into his arms and placed her on his bed. This was it. The moment to give her some space. He leaned in to kiss her cheek, but she grabbed his collar, forcing him to meet her eye. "Kiss my lips, Micah Henry, or don't kiss me at all."

He traced his fingers up her forearm, leaving a trail of icy goosebumps blooming in their wake, stopping only when his thumb caressed the curve of her collarbone. "The last time we kissed, we started a war."

"And you did what you do best. You left all of us."

He pressed his lips to her forehead. It had been so long. He wondered if she was merely a mirage. "I came back," he said quietly. "I came back, didn't I?"

"And what did it take for us to get this closure, Micah?"

Closure. Those words haunted him. Closure signified an end. It signified moving on. He was not ready to move on. He wrestled the melancholy penetrating his skull as unsolicited visitors do, fighting to regain custody over his emotions. The word closure echoing in his head, he relented to his hollowness and came to the same conclusion he had reached countless times before: he couldn't do this, not today. It was easier to claim he never loved her then to abandon her in the aftermath.

"Do you have it then?" he asked her. "Closure?"

"Is that what you want for us? Closure?"

He sat on the edge of his bed, saying nothing.

She lifted her head despite her humiliation, his silence stinging like shrapnel against her bare skin. "God, Micah, loving you like this hurts," she said all too quickly. And when he said nothing, she shook her head ironically, as if in disbelief by his actions—or once again, lack thereof. "I said loving you hurts, you fucking idiot."

He sat there, his mind a whirlwind of indecipherable thoughts.

"And maybe I don't love you as much as I love the idea of you," she continued. "But fucking hell, every time I see you, you make me relive that night all over again. How much longer are you going to do this to me? How much longer before it's enough for you?"

He recoiled. She loved him. After all these years, she still loved him.

"Sol," Micah breathed, like it was the most wistful serenade he had ever sung. And when he met her eyes, he did it so longingly, like he would do anything to be in this one moment for all of eternity. And who knows what possessed him then, as he grabbed her waist and pressed her against his bed frame, her thighs trembling above his unflinching grasp. An unchaste moan escaped her lips as he pressed his lips into hers, their bodies dancing as if they were not at risk of decay. And they pretended, in the fleeting moment that manifested, that Micah was not destined to die.

When she tried to pull away, he wouldn't let her—and Sol saw why. His eyes glistened, withholding his guilty tears. "How could you love me, Sol?" he trembled against her lips. "I don't have much time. I could go. Any minute now."

She bit his lip in an anguished effort to silence him. Placing a hand upon his beating heart, she shook her head against his own. "Stop this, bubba. You're not dead yet, are you?"

"I'd need a miracle."

"You're alive, Micah. And you are loved so much more than you can ever imagine. Isn't that your miracle?

He opened his eyes, wishing for the first time that he hadn't left her on that boardwalk all those months ago. Because she was right, you see. This love—it was his miracle.

CHAPTER 17

We boarded a flight to Monroe Hills early the next morning, the halfway point between San City and Holden. The familiar monoliths of cascading concrete diminished into the barren wastelands we knew best: thousands of acres of outstretched land, abandoned and untended to, intermittently disrupted by a faint glimmer of civilization. A waning crescent hovering in the periphery of the panoramic sky, we landed quietly with the town submerged in its nightly slumber.

With the exception of a few solitary travelers, Lara, Mama, Ezra and I were the only ones to land in the airport. The vicinity was quaint and desolate, with empty conveyor belts incessantly spinning and security personnel nowhere to be found. We followed the signs to the connecting train station. Ezra and I shared a bar of Kinder as we sped past Mama on the moving walkways. Clara shook her head, murmuring something akin to "How you two have this much energy at four in the morning is beyond me," while we laughed, racing past one another as if in a race against time. Lethargic from a lack of sleep with only our laughter to entertain us, we exited into the station.

"Eerie much?" Clara said as we stepped onto the platform.

My laughter subsided at the sight before me: the station, vacant and somber, with derelict street lamps housing its dim, flickering lights. "Are you sure we're in the right place?"

"We should be," Mama said. She looked behind her shoulder. "Ezra?"

Ezra pulled out his phone for a glimpse at what I assumed was the map, only to release a sigh. He held it up. "No service."

"Maybe we can ask a station master?" I offered, looking around for a hut.

Clara chuckled. "See any station masters around, love?"

"I guess not. When's the train getting here anyway?"

"Five thirty," Mama said.

"That gives us—"

Ezra glanced at his watch. "One hour and twenty three minutes."

We walked along the platform, discovering for ourselves the brittle silence that blankets Monroe Hills at four a.m. I looked around for an indication that we were in the right place to board the five thirty train to Holden. We stopped along a bench, dropping our luggages and taking a seat, Clara burying her chin in her palms. "Five thirty to Holden. Wake me up, will you, Ez?"

He bit his lip, pulling his earphones out of his pocket. "Of course, Lar," he said. He opened his music player, sliding one of his buds into my ear. "We've got to pass the time somehow, right?" he said, looking at me.

I rested my chin on my palms, observing him as he navigated his playlists: The White Stripes, The Velvet Underground, Honne, Earth Dad and other independent artists I did not recognize.

"You kids stay here," Mama said in the meantime. "I'm going to figure out if we're on the right platform and maybe grab some breakfast."

I nodded at Mama, brushing her off.

Ezra nudged me lightly. "Any suggestions, Narns?"

"Whatever you want."

A small smile graced his face. "How about this?"

At his words, a steady melody began to play—a mellow song, a lullaby under the velvet light of the stars as my legs sought solace on top of Ezra's, the confluence of our bodies providing a momentary fortress from the cold.

He placed an elbow on my thigh, resting his chin on his palms. "Thoughts?"

In the heart of that forsaken town,

Where we were never blue,

Where orchards bloomed like no other,

And we never quite knew

What tomorrow held for us...

I'm tired, baby, you would say,

Tired, I was too,

But never of loving you

In our little old town,

The glory of our youth

"It reminds me of us," I said.

"Yeah?"

"Yeah. Of our own old little town—you know? Of Holden."

"How did we let a place like Holden carry our glory days?"

"That was just our luck, wasn't it?"

"Maybe. But it'll get better. I have this feeling, Narnie, that when we go back, nothing is going to be as it was. I'm not going to be in that rundown trailer anymore. We'll move to San City, Clara and I. And you'll come—for university, you know? And we'll build our lives again, from scratch. We'll leave everything behind."

"Is that really what you want, Ezra? To leave everything behind?"

"Everything but you," he said, brushing his lips against mine. The gesture quelled the words forming on my tongue. "We'll do everything. We'll go to Beirut, Annapurna—Meteora. We're going to make it, Narnie, you and me. We'll grow old. I can already see it. Me reading you Tolstoy at seventy and you'll be the sexiest seventy year old woman this world has ever seen. I'll seduce you with my words even in old age."

"Someday," I whispered into his lips.

He enclosed what existed of the proximity between us. "Someday."

I pulled away and rested my head on his shoulder, closing my eyes as he pulled out a copy of The Book of Disquiet to keep him company. I must have fallen asleep like that, with nothing to blanket me but the occasional brushing of our bodies. When I woke up a little later, he was still there, his eyes wandering the platitudes in his book. I sat up to find Clara no longer there.

"She went to find a bathroom," Ezra said, as if reading my mind.

I outstretched my arms to loosen the knots forming in them. "When's the train coming?"

"Still forty seven more minutes to go."

"Did Mama come back?"

"No, but I think we're at the right place," he said. He motioned toward a man standing on the edge of the platform, in his several day stubble, impenetrable winter jacket and a pair of washed away jeans. A duffle bag resting between his legs, his eyes remained tethered to the side of the station from which the train was expected to arrive.

"Should I go ask him? Just to be sure?"

"Whatever you want, Narns," he said, flipping to another page in his novel.

I approached him cautiously, this mysterious man on the platform, taking in his unfaltering gaze, still glued to the distance as if engrossed in a deep calculation. "Excuse me," I began to say, but when he turned around, his hands trembled to his forehead. It was then that I saw it: the gun, resting between his fingers, distraught with uncertainty as it faltered at his constricting temples. Beneath the awakening sky, branches writhed like claws of ravenous beasts. Imaginary monsters manifested in the wintry air, distilling the little of my remaining calmness.

"Ezra," I croaked out, my voice a bare whisper, as I took a step backwards.

The stranger looked behind me at the emerging figure of Clara Parker, a solitary tear sliding down his vacant eyes. "This is my testimony, Clara Parker."

He swallowed before his fingers pressed the trigger. I snapped my eyes shut in anticipation of his blood defiling my skin, but it never came. My ears instead processed an explosion: the sound of a bullet entering an innocent body. When I opened my eyes, everything came crashing down as I saw Ezra's body falling limply to the ground.

I may have sobbed—screamed. In some recollections, I develop four hands and save him. The stranger then took the gun and disgraced Hemingway with a successful shot to his own head, his listless body collapsing onto the forgotten tracks, now carrying a forgotten soul, his vices neither forgotten nor penanced.

The accent of sirens cleaved the stillness like a needle entering a carcass. The violence of Clara's cries arresting the vicinity, we trust four bodies into the ambulance car the moment Mama arrived, Clara's breathing the only audible one. We discovered when we entered the hospital that we had lost three souls instead of two, the vigor in Clara's eyes now lost to the callous determinism of her destiny. Maybe this was the universe, recompensing for her vices. She had often taken her life for granted. She was foolish, free, rebellious—the epitome of careless. And her carelessness had cost her her brother.

He appeared into the scene like an otherworldly being, providing no indication nor declaration. He did not even issue a warning of what his presence would entail. He may have been the wind, a caress or a ghost, invading others' most precious convictions and still haunting mine like a ruthless despot. If he desired an empire, he achieved it with me, for I would carve out every skin on my body and hand it over as states to his greater nation.

An hour after we arrived at the hospital, his heart monitor stopped beeping—and I realized that I had never told him that I loved him. I murmured I love you's until I numbed myself to what those words meant. I kissed his pale lips and trembled through the motion, feeling the remaining of my livelihood being sucked out of my being. "What about Beirut, Ezra?" I stammered through my numbness. "What about being seventy?" If I had a volition—a will—to live, he took it with him that very night when he left me for the unknown.

CHAPTER 18

His name was Caleb Frazier, but the world knew him as Jestem Matar, a brooding Renaissance man with a penchant for historic art. To us, he was no different from the other outcasts roaming our town, but on Carrie Becker's radio show, he was a sensation.

"According to news making headlines around America this morning, police have captured a man tied to several murders, from Monroe Hills to Port Orion. Most recently tied to the murder of eighteen year old Ezra Parker, the suspect, Caleb Frazier, is said to have murdered Mr. Parker in plain sight and have taken his own life shortly after..."

Tuning out the static interfering with her voice, I lay on my bed, recounting the countless news reports preceding her's. An earlier segment featuring Katie Rosenlicht had revealed that Frazier had never intended to kill Ezra that day. He had left behind a note for the Holden sheriff department before his departure to Monroe Hills, admitting to his vices. In it, he'd written that he'd had enough; that he was done with the murders; that he was driving to the platform in Monroe Hills known for its desolation, to shoot himself in front of the five thirty to Holden.

So we had been in the wrong place at the wrong time. Was that it? Was that really it? If we had boarded a later plane into town, Ezra would still be here? He would still be with me?

"He had said he would do this, Narnie," Clara had sobbed in the car ride to the hospital, referring to the stranger, Jestem. "He had said that if I ever ran away, if I ever reported him, he would take away everything and everyone that I held dear." Her words rang in my ears until they became indecipherable.

Ezra Parker. I tried to consider what life was like before him—I really did—but he had slipped into my every memory, even the ones preceding his arrival that day in late August. Late August. When moths swarmed the lampposts and the sultry smell of sweat varnished the air. When I crossed paths with Ezra Parker for the very first time, convinced that this time, it would be different—that he would be infinite. But even Ezra Parker could not survive the thread of death. This inevitability—this was the plight of the human condition.

I sighed, thinking about his last words, about how hopeful he had been. He had been so sure that things were going to change. It was the universe's greatest act of cruelty, filling him with a sense of beginning just moments before his end.

And the days passed, one after another. The day of his funeral, it rained savagely. I was in my room, applying concealer and listening to Carrie Becker's reporting on Amira Parker's case. Murdered in cold blood by Jestem Matar while sedated in her bedroom with a benzodiazepine she hadn't known she had ingested. It happened on a Sunday, after a fight with her husband. She was in the bar, an empty bar, when Jestem approached her—and because Ezra's father had been the last to see her, because the sheriffs had found benzodiazepine on their nightstand and her dead body in their house, he had been taken away as the suspect. I didn't realize I was crying until Mama slipped into my room. Hearing the interference ricocheting in between Carrie Becker's words and my sobs, she reached for the radio. "I'm turning it off, Narnie."

I dabbed my eyelashes with a tissue, careful not to ruin my makeup.

"Have you eaten?"

I eyed the lentil soup she had brought up just an hour ago, now cold. Its insipid brown took me back to that morning: to the blood pooling out of Jestem's head, brown in the eternal darkness. It was this same brown that had pumped his veins as he stripped me of my new beginning. I thought about his bloodstains, fresh against my face, and felt the nausea taking over. I reached for my trashcan, gagging out the little of the soup I had eaten, wishing that I could purge myself of him instead.

Mama stood on the edge of my vanity, gently massaging my hair. "Baby, I'm here, I'm here..."

"How am I supposed to do this, Mama?" I sputtered out. "How am I supposed to bury him?"

"Oh, Narnie..."

"He wasn't supposed to leave us so soon. How could he be gone—just like that—just like Papa?"

"It isn't a permanent goodbye, baby. He's waiting for you in heaven."

"You act like there are no pretty girls in heaven."

"None of them are you, my sweet Narnie."

"Narnie Larson?" an unfamiliar man repeated just hours later, at his son's funeral. His eyes the same green, he approached me cautiously as Larisa gave her parting remarks behind the podium in the funeral home.

I looked at the man. Did I know him?

"Oh, where are my manners? I'm Clarence, Clarence Parker."

I softened my glare, swallowing the champagne I was gurgling in my mouth. "Mr. Parker."

His lips formulated a weak smile, one that didn't quite reach his eyes. "Call me Clarence."

"I'm sorry, Clarence."

"Sorry?"

"Sorry that I couldn't save him."

"Oh, Narnie, dear..."

I felt my breathing labor.

"You were his best friend."

Then why did he leave me, Mr. Parker? Why did he abandon his best friend? I wanted to ask. I sighed instead, stealing a fleeting glance at his cadaver until I couldn't anymore. "I just can't believe he's really gone."

Mr. Parker smiled again, this smile weaker than the one before. "How can he be gone? You love him so much."

I swallowed the lump growing in my throat.

"Narnie?"

"Yeah?"

He reached for something in his inside coat pocket. "We were clearing out the caravan, Clara and I—and we found this."

I looked at the familiar blue on his hand: Hermann Hesse's Siddhartha.

"It seems to be your copy. I found your name on the inside cover."

I took it from him and opened it to the title page. And there it was: my name, written in my own handwriting, with Ezra's familiar script leading up to it: Life is an endless light with you, Narnie Larson.

I closed the book, squeezing my eyes shut. And when I opened them, tears were pooling down my face like never before. "Excuse me," I said, brushing past Mr. Parker. I exited the venue and entered the lady's room, finding Sol fixing her running makeup.

I rushed up to her, burying my face in her neck. She held me without a word, her silence my sanctuary until my tears ran dry. I cried for Ezra and I cried for her. I cried for the cruelty this world put us through: for the casualties of war and famine. I cried for the possibilities severed by fate. I cried in protest against death. How could I not?

There were times in our lives when we encountered a connection so powerful that it left us completely transformed. All it took was a second, a minute or a day, after which we were never the same again. We are told that true love is nurtured with time—that we do not know a person enough to truly love them until a year and sometimes five. This is a myth. Because I fell in love with Ezra Parker overnight. And maybe it was what we never were that is more enchanting than the days we lived to see. But I found myself entranced by his familiar magic—by the way he could, with a simple glance, read my heart's language.

I worried that I would grow old and no longer remember him. As I saw his face amid the warfare I waged against forgetting, I harnessed the freedom I once felt when I was in love, a freedom I feared could be imprisonment with the wrong person—and I cried more at the possibility that I would never love again.

Bella entered the room not much later, finding the two of us. She hesitated, reaching for her phone before wrapping her arms around my waist. A little later, we were joined by Anderson, Micah and Teo, who enveloped me in their tighter embrace. Then it was just the six of us, standing in the middle of the lady's room in that quiet suburban morning, crying softly for the loss of someone who had become a part of us, someone we were condemned to live on without.

CHAPTER 19

The days passed by the way they knew best, uncaring of our grief. As the winter's cruel bite faded into March's gentle caress, the once barren suburban wastelands gave way to the perennial hope of spring. Even then, I found in myself only a greater darkness, a darkness that led me to wonder how the world could be so apathetic to the cruelties it subjected us to. I wondered why we had not yet evolved out of our tendency to feel so hollow, why our biology thought that was worth preserving—and I wondered why Ezra's ghost followed me everywhere I went, why I could not move on.

I trudged along the field, exiting the arena after one of our most important games of the season. He would be so proud if he was here, to see his boys win against the San City Sea Dragons. The entire world had been watching, awaiting Holden's defeat, but Anderson had taken the field by a storm in the final minutes of the game. With little time for the Sea Dragons to recover, it was done. The underdogs had won.

How would we celebrate if you were still here, Ezra? Would we go on another one of our infamous drives across Holden? Would we find a cliffside to sit by, get high and speculate about what the future held? Would we sit on the very edge, our feet dangling the air, as I poured onto you my foolish jurisdictions about love—about how far I had come since back then? How I was leaving for San City in less than three months for university, how I was winning the war against forgetting—how I was certain I would never forget you, not even in old age when met with a fate of delirium.

A sense of foreboding jolted me into reality as taut arms grabbed me by my knees, swinging me into the air. "And just where do you think you're going, Larson?"

It took me a second to register the familiar blonde hair. Anderson. Behind us, the sound of Bella's laughter filled the vicinity. I smiled weakly at him. "Please put me down, Anderson."

"Bella, she's moping again."

"I am not."

"You totally are."

"I'm not."

"You are."

"Bella, tell him to put me down."

"Put her down, Anderson."

He tossed me over his shoulders. "Never."

As he turned us around, I caught a glimpse of Teo walking beside Bella. "Good game Teo," I said.

"Thank you, Narnie bear."

Anderson shook his head. "Wow, Narnie. Just make it a little more obvious you like Teo more than me."

Bella rolled her eyes. "Everyone likes Teo more than you, Andy."

"Even you?"

Bella looked away, her cheeks reddening. Sol slipped between her and Teo, making herself known. "Micah texted! He's pulling up."

Anderson chuckled. "Do you two ever stop texting?"

"Yeah, when we go to sleep, duh."

"You two don't sleep," Bella pointed out.

"What do you even talk about at this point?" Anderson asked.

Sol shrugged. "N.O.Y.B."

"N.O.Y.B?"

"None of your business."

"Oh, wow. So witty. Wow."

As the two continued to bicker, Micah pulled into the parking lot. Sol rushed up to him as he exited his car, engulfing him in a hug. "Baby!"

He chuckled, rubbing the back of her neck. "Hi, Solita."

She held his hands in trepidation, maybe fearing that he would disappear. He would soon. Any day now.

"Relax, Sol," Anderson said. "Let the guy breathe."

She glared at him, forcing him to look away.

Bella shook her head in amusement. "When did she get like this?"

Anderson placed me on the ground, following her gaze. "You're asking me?"

"As long as she's happy, right?" Teo said quietly.

"Happy?" Bella repeated. "She's fucking mad."

She was—and it wasn't just Sol, but Micah too. It was like they existed in another plane, detached from the rest of us. When it was just the two of them, it was as if we vanished into thin air, like we were merely white noise fading to oblivion. And as the days unraveled, Micah had found that it was not death that had creeped up on him, but the tenacity of his life, demanding his agency. He wrapped his arms around Sol, resting his chin on her head. "Ready to go, Bella?"

"Are you?"

He brought his face down to Sol's. "You ready, baby?"

She nodded.

We loaded ourselves into the car, Bella, Anderson, Teo and I squeezing into the backseat. I wedged myself between the boys as Bella sat on the edge of Anderson's knee. As the car gathered motion, he wrapped his arms around her waist, pulling her into his lap. We pulled away from the parking lot, where hundreds of lives had intersected without our slightest clue, each life parallel to the other until they weren't anymore. And I looked at the people around me—at Micah and Sol, with their fingers entwined, at Anderson and Bella, fighting over who got the auxiliary cord and at Teo, shaking his head at the two as he disconnected his phone from the bluetooth—thinking about how easily we could have missed each other—how fortunate we were that we didn't.

I leaned closer to the driver's seat. "Hey Micah?"

"Yeah?"

"Where are we going?"

"It's a surprise."

Teo turned his head to the two of us. "A surprise? Is there an occasion?"

"No," Micah said, squeezing Sol's hand. "No occasion."

"Are we almost there?" Bella asked, wriggling for more room on top of Anderson.

"We literally just got in the car, Bels," Anderson said.

"I'm sorry, Anderson. Did I ask you?"

"You asked somebody."

"Do me a favor and stop talking to me."

"Bella—"

"How many more minutes, Micah?" Bella demanded.

"Elevenish," Micah said.

Anderson wrapped his head around her arm, pouting his lips. "Bella?"

"Did I not just ask you to stop talking to me?"

"I didn't say anything," Anderson said in his defense.

"You just said Bella."

"That was Micah."

"Anderson, I literally saw you."

"Whatever you say, Bella."

Bella sunk back into him, softening her glare. As Micah merged into the highway, the familiar melody of Pinkish Sunrise drifted out of his speakers. I took in the sweet discomfort of being in this space, where physical boundaries ceased to exist against the realization that I was surrounded by the people I loved most in this world—people with whom I had become one.

Bella sighed, playing with the edges of her fingers.

"Don't be so bloody moody, Bella," Micah said, glancing at her from his rearview mirror.

"I'm not moody."

"She says in the voice of death," Teo said with a chuckle.

"Why would I be moody? Like, what reason do I have?"

Teo and I exchanged glances.

"Whatever," Bella huffed, crossing her arms across her chest. "This conversation is over."

I wondered how long she would go on like this: how many more times she would fall in love with Anderson until they saw it in each other's eyes at last. We arrived along our destination quicker than anticipated. The vacant roads gave way to the sea, its body scattering the setting sky like glittering stars on a violet night.

The boys reached for the tote bags in the trunk as Micah parked the car. Sol exited first, followed by Teo, Anderson and Bella. I watched from the backseat as they laid sheets on the bare stand, unloading the bags and picnic baskets.

"Did you plan all of this for us?" I asked Micah, motioning toward the bags.

"We did, Narnie—for you."

"For me?"

As Sol closed the door to the trunk, Micah took his keys off the ignition. "Let's go."

I exited the car to the fresh smell of seawater. A lavender sky above, coral waves crashed against the gravel wearing by the shore. Laid out on Micah's sheets were wine glasses, spirits, bread, cheese assortments and a wooden board filled with chopped lychees, mangoes, clementines and guavas. I removed my sandals and pressed my bare feet on the sand. And when I sat down to Bella removing her tres leches cake with We r so proud of u Narnie written in frosting, I felt in me an irresistible desire to cry.

Sol fumbled through the tote bags. "Micah, did you put the candle in here?"

"Uh, was I supposed to do that?"

"Ugh, Micah!"

"Just kidding," he said, pulling one out of his jacket pocket.

I sniffled, just a little, sitting down next to Bella. "We could've gone without the candles anyway."

"Narnie," Bella murmured, reaching for my hands.

"I'm sorry. I'm just really emotional right now."

Teo wrapped his arms around me, pulling me close. "We're here, Narns."

"I just—I love you guys so much."

"We love you too, Narnie," Sol said softly. "We love you so much."

"I love you too, Sol."

Micah slid the candle into the cake and lit it. "Make a wish, Larson."

I wish Ezra was still here.

Bella faltered.

"Fuck, did I just say that out loud?"

"Yes, you did, Narnie," Bella said quietly.

"Don't look so blue, Bels," Anderson said. "His name is not the plague."

"It's just—it's only been a few months. Narnie, are you ready?"

"I think so. I read online that it takes 66 days to get over an old habit. It's been more, right?"

Sol scoffed, glancing at Micah. "As if."

"Is that your wish then?" Bella asked. "The candle is starting to drip."

I looked around me at everyone's wide, anticipating eyes. Maybe that would be a wasted wish, to wish for him to come back. I sighed. I hope that we all make it—that we find ourselves happy, wherever we go, I amended. I closed my eyes and blew the candle. As the fumes drifted into the air, Anderson scooped the frosting on the edge of the tray with his fingers and planted it on the tip of Bella's nose.

She narrowed her eyes at him as he said, "Can I lick it off, Bella? It looks so yummy."

"You are a child," she said, reaching for a napkin.

"You abuse me."

"You deserve it."

"How do I deserve it?"

Bella scowled, dividing the cake into slices.

"How do I deserve it, Bels?"

"Shut up for a minute."

He reached for a clementine, his cheeks slightly red. Just then, when he was the most unsuspecting, she took a large slice of the cake and planted it on his head.

His eyes widened. "For fuck's sake, Bella."

"Can I lick it off, Anderson? It looks so yummy."

Micah looked at the two in amusement. "Are they always like this?"

Sol followed his gaze sheepishly. "This is them on a good day."

"Do I want to see them on a bad day?"

"Tame your curiosity, Micah."

"It's that bad?"

"It?" Bella repeated, darting her head towards Micah. "Who are you calling it?"

Anderson tugged her shoulder. "Hey Bels?"

"Yeah?"

"You want to go for a swim?"

"With you?"

He grabbed her wrist, pulling her into him. "Please?"

She shoved him away, softening. "Fine. Race you there?"

He nodded, watching Bella as she removed her dress, revealing only her undergarments. We watched them disappear until they were just avatars in the horizon.

"How long until they figure it out?" Sol asked us.

"However long it took us times a hundred," Micah said wistfully.

"I guess stubbornness runs in the family."

"I came around, didn't I?"

Sol smiled weakly, standing up and cleaning up the trail of cake Anderson had left behind.

Micah looked at her. "Walk with me?"

She stopped what she was doing and circled behind him, wrapping her arms around his neck. "Only if you carry me."

And he did. As Micah and Sol wandered away, Teo took a clementine from the tray.

I frowned at him. "You okay, Teo?"

"Yeah," he said. "Why wouldn't I be?"

"You've just been really quiet."

"Just thinking."

"About?"

"How we don't have much time left. How in just a few months, we're all going to go our separate ways."

"Teo..."

"I got into Cambridge."

"Cambridge? Like, Cambridge Cambridge?"

He nodded.

I smiled so widely that I wondered if I could smile any more. "Look at you."

"Thanks, Narns. But I still feel so lost—I don't know. I miss him."

"I miss him too."

"Did you figure out what you're doing yet?"

"Does anyone ever figure out what they're doing?"

"Good point."

"I deferred my acceptance to San City. They were okay with it. I'll probably take a semester off before starting that philosophy degree."

"In San City?"

"Yeah."

"I admire you."

I raised an eyebrow at him, resisting a scoff. "Who? Me?"

"Yeah, you. There's just something about you. We were a mess before you came into our lives. We were all kind of gliding through the motions, half-asleep, but then you came, so full of life and so much agency. It's like you threaded us back together."

"Thank you, Teo, but I really didn't do anything."

"You gave us hope."

Had I? Had I really given them hope? Because they had given me hope.

Micah came back not much later, a guitar slung over his shoulders and Sol's hand in his. As he sat down and began plucking the strings, the sound of Bella's laughter filled the air. It sounded closer and closer until she was with us again, drying her body with a towel. She handed it to Anderson when she was done, taking a seat beside us.

"Fuck, Micah," Sol said as Micah played a Frankie Vallie song. I had heard it before, in one of her memories. She looked so happy that the melody warmed me up as if it was my own.

"Sing for me?" Micah said.

She blushed, but she did, lying down and sliding her head to his lap. As the song ended, we lapsed into a momentary silence with nothing but the lapping waves to pacify us.

"We should still do it, you know?" I finally said, taking everyone by surprise. When five pairs of curious eyes landed on me, I looked away at the sea. "We should still go to Beirut. We should go to Annapurna. Maybe not anytime soon, but someday—someday we should all go."

"Someday," Sol said with a sigh.

"Yeah, someday," Teo echoed wistfully.

Micah removed his guitar from his lap, placing it on the empty space beside him.

"You should play, Andy," Bella said, grabbing it before it could stay on the floor for too long. She inched it towards him. "Come on."

He hesitated. "Bella, I—"

"Go on, Flemming," Micah said. "Serenade us like you used to."

He sat there for the longest time, doing nothing, until Bella slid closer to him and gently placed the guitar on his lap, moving his fingers to the frets. "Please?" she said quietly.

He looked between the guitar and the love of his life, between her and his best friends, between us and the sea. Without another word, he began to play.

EPILOGUE

I am going back to the place where it all began. For the first time in eternity, I am engulfed by the endless blue of the horizon. Around me, day is just falling, illuminating the expressway with the pacifying light of morning. I unroll my windows, taking in the crisp early summer breeze. The sensation is nostalgic, like I am on a motorcycle instead of an encased Sedan. My navigator advises me to take the next exit and when I do, I am there; I am back in the place where it all began.

I have only visited this place in stories—this worn out diner in the heart of Fort Montgomery where Sol and Micah fell in love for the first time, before he had left us for his final adventure. Now I am here and when I close my eyes, I can envision it all. I can envision Ezra.

"Holy shit," a familiar voice breathes. He staggers as if I am a ghost. "Look who it is."

I look up and I see Teo. He has matured significantly since the last time I saw him. He looks better now than he ever has, at twenty six. I pull him into a hug, one that unbinds all of my nostalgia for him to hold. "Fuck, I've missed you," I say, holding back the tears already threatening to fall from my eyes.

"I've missed you too," he says. He holds me firmly, hesitating before pulling away. "Everyone's already inside. We were waiting for you."

"How is everyone?"

"Bella's engaged."

"Really?"

"Yeah. She's happy; I'm happy."

"I guess we're all in a better place now, aren't we?"

"We really are," he says. With that, he leads me inside. The place is everything I imagined it would be. It is that and more.

I savor the soft melody emerging from the jukebox as Teo navigates our way across the quaint vicinity. The place is so empty that I wonder if the universe has reserved it for just the five of us today. It is then that I see her—Bella—and I suddenly feel such a torrent of emotions that I begin to cry. She looks so beautiful in her orange sundress. In that moment, we are still seventeen and have yet to experience the adversities life has to offer. We are still foolish; we are still naïve; we are still daydreaming about Ezra Parker with nothing but our hearts on our sleeves.

As she turns around, I cannot help but recount every single one of our memories, starting from our very first day in the highway to our evenings by the Hudson, with only Micah and Sol's makeout sessions to entertain us. There is a soft melancholy that accompanies the memories because I know I can never relive them. They are infinitely gone. I rely on my heart to hold their permanence.

She screams the moment she sees me, running towards me for an overdue embrace. We are suddenly laughing and crying and when we draw apart, we are twenty six and blue again.

"Just when were you going to tell me you're engaged, Bella Henry?"

She wipes her watery eyes with her index finger, biting her lip. "I wanted to surprise you."

"Oh my god," I say, taking in her glistening engagement ring.

"It's beautiful, right? Anderson picked it."

"How did he do it? How did he propose?"

She blushes. She has the eyes I had at seventeen, when I had yet to grow so cynical about love. I hope she never does.

"So we're both out grocery shopping, right?" she begins. "And I'm complaining like a madwoman because things have been really shitty at work. And we're by the checkout line and he tells me very secretively that he knows something that can make me feel better. I tell him nothing can make me feel better. And that's when he does it. He goes on one knee and asks me to marry him and I drop my fucking egg carton because I'm so shocked."

I imagine it in my head. That is the most Anderson thing to do: to take a mundane place and to turn it into the sublime. It warms my heart.

"I love him so much," she says breathlessly. She looks ready to cry again, as if the passion of love is too great for her to bear. It is then that Anderson slides beside her, a mischievous smile illuminating his face.

"Who's this stranger?" he says teasingly.

"Can't say we've met before," I say with a shrug.

He chuckles, enveloping me in a hug. "It's good to see you, Narnie."

I take in his familiar smell, wondering how he can smell the same after all these years. I am about to cry again when a familiar voice calls my name. "Narnie?"

I turn around and I see Clara. It is painful to see her after all these years. I am looking at her but all I can see is him. As she fills the space before me with her green eyes, I find every bone in my body aching with a dizzying urge to see him again.

"Clara," I say weakly. "How are you?"

"I've been okay. I hear you're good though, that you're seeing someone?"

"On and off," I say. I resist the part of me that wants to say Nothing really seems to last these days, but it is true. Even though it has been years, it still feels as if I have been measuring every man I meet against Ezra, against his curiosity, his passion—his free spirit. Some days, I wonder if he has imperialized every space of my nostalgic memory, such that no one can enter it ever again. Love is ruthless in that way; it does not reveal what cruelties are concealed in its depth until it is lost for the first time.

"Whoever he is, he's a lucky man," she says, tearing me away from my thoughts. She peers into me again with those green eyes. "You're my sister, aren't you?"

"Of course, Clara," I say. "What about you? Where's Alex?"

"He's on his way from Granada."

"Granada?"

"Yeah. Business trip. Can you believe I married a corporate sellout?"

"We all have weaknesses," I say—but it makes me happy to hear that he is successful now. He has left his old life behind and that is all I ever wanted for him.

"I suppose," she says with a smile. "Have you spoken to Sol yet?"

Sol Flores. Now that is a name I haven't heard in a while. It is also a name I will never forget, one I will remember even when old age kicks in and I am met with a fate of delirium.

"She was looking forward to seeing you," Clara adds. "She's backstage if you want to see her."

"I will. Thank you," I say. I find her exactly where I expect to, leaning against the wall and sipping a cup of coffee. At the noise of my arrival, she raises her head. There is shock. There is hesitance. Then there is acceptance.

"Narnie fucking Larson," she says, her voice wavering.

I walk in, resisting a smile. "Sol fucking Flores."

"Someone looks like they haven't gotten laid in a while."

"Eight years apart and that's all you have to say to me?"

She laughs—but she has resurfaced memories I have long tucked away, memories of Ezra and I and that afternoon in Clara's bedroom, when his sighs had pacified the night as our bodies coalesced for the first and last time. It was with him that I learned human beings could truly fly.

"How are you, Narnie?" she digresses, her voice grounding me from my nostalgia.

"I finally finished law school," I say softly.

"I saw the pictures on Instagram. Starting a clerkship soon?"

"Yeah, right when I get back to San City. Specializing in criminal justice."

"Ezra's going to appreciate that one day."

I laugh a little, the gesture melancholy. "Yeah."

"Yeah," she says quietly.

"What about you? What have you been up to?"

"I've been up in Boston finishing my PhD."

"A PhD. Wow."

"Yeah, decided to study quantum mechanics. Trying to come up with a formula to rewind time."

"You sentimental bitch."

"I couldn't help it. I just—"

"He set a high bar. I understand."

"It's not that. It's just that being with anyone else feels like betrayal, you know? I want to. But I emotionally can't."

"Sol—"

"It's okay. I told myself I wouldn't be overly sentimental tonight. Is everyone here?"

"Everyone except Alex?" I say skeptically. "I didn't know he was coming."

"Anderson invited him and Clara."

"I don't know why I thought it was going to be just the five of us."

"The more the merrier, I guess."

"Did they book their flights?"

She nods. Just then a song begins to play. Pinkish Sunrise. I feel in me another pang of nostalgia, but I suppress it as we exit back into the venue. It is then I see him: Alex Lewinsky, standing by the entrance. I don't know why, but seeing him is my restoration. I greet him with a wave. "Missed you, Lewinsky!"

He grins in that distinctly Alex way of his. "Missed you more."

"Heard you've been telling Clara all about me."

"Of course. King of gossip here. Don't you remember?"

I laugh. It feels so good to laugh like this. I wonder why I ever stopped.

"Is everyone here?" Clara asks, looking between Alex and Bella.

Bella turns to Anderson. "Sweetie, is Roman coming?"

"He should be."

As if on cue, he arrives then—this mysterious Roman. His hair is damp, indicating that it has begun to rain. As our eyes meet, I realize that I have met him before, in Sol's memories. I meet him again like I have never been in love, like I am approaching existence for the very first time.

"So this is Roman," I say cheekily.

He smiles, his dimples sinking the skin on his cheek. "Anderson, you didn't say there were going to be pretty girls on this trip."

Clara laughs, shaking her head. "Someone hasn't changed."

He walks closer toward her and lifts her in a hug. "Hi, Lara bear."

"For fuck's sake, Roman."

"So how are we doing this?" Sol asks, glancing at Bella. "Are we taking an Uber or—"

"What about my car?" I begin to say, to which Anderson laughs.

"There's no way we'd all fit. We're leaving ours in the lot until we're back."

"In the lot? For three weeks? Is that safe?"

"Maybe Uncle Edem is plotting an elaborate plan to steal all our cars," Clara chimes in.

I roll my eyes. "Ha, ha, ha Clara. Very funny."

"Seriously though, it should be fine, love," she says. "I doubt anyone will even notice."

I nod. It is Holden after all.

We end up calling an Uber. It is the only way we can all fit in one car. The journey to the airport is fleeting. Somehow, our waiting time for our flight is even shorter, ending as we board the 10:30 a.m. to Nepal. We arrive in Kathmandu later than expected, but just in time for our seven hour bus ride from the valley to Annapurna.

We had planned this so long ago that I can hardly believe we are actually here. Our someday is now today, where the road is paved with jagged pathways and coated in virgin snow. I close my eyes and take it in. A sense of appreciation for the world and this very existence overwhelms me.

When I open my eyes again, I see Ezra. He is extending his hand for me to take, for we have reached our destination. I take it and let him lead me into the wilderness, where a new life is waiting for me.

Against the subtle cries of nature, I find peace. I find home. I find the past and the future strung into a present that is demanding to be lived. I find that in spite of my agony, I am still alive. And when I close my eyes in the impermanent moments that face their death and rebirth, so is he.

www.ingramcontent.com/pod-product-compliance
Lightning Source LLC
Chambersburg PA
CBHW070939190726
48292CB00004B/1254